FATED MAGIC

SHADOW COVEN
BOOK THREE

USA TODAY BESTSELLING AUTHOR

HEATHER YOUNG-NICHOLS

Fated Magic
The Shadow Coven Book 3
Heather Young-Nichols

heatheryoungnichols.com

ALSO BY HEATHER YOUNG-NICHOLS

Shadow Coven

Haunted Magic

Cursed Magic

Stolen Magic

Fated Magic

Forever 18

Forever Grayson

Forever London

Forever Lennox

Heavy Hitter

Pushing Daisies

Daisy

Van

Bonham

Daltrey

Mack

Courting Chaos

Cross

Ransom

Booker

Dixon

Finding Love

Making Her Mine

Making Him Hers

Harbor Point

Love by the Slice

Love by the Mile

Love by the Rules

Gambling on Love

Highest Bidder

Highest Stakes

Highest Reward

Holiday Bites

All I Want

All of Me

The Fallout Series

Last Good Thing

Last First Kiss

Last Chance Love

With J.A. Hardt

Bound by Magic

With Amelia J. Matthews

Dirt on the Diamond

After Office Hours: Seducing the Professor

1

MILLER

THE FOUR OF us stood waiting for the attack.

Our group had barely arrived at the cabin my father sent us to before this dark witch showed up. The women were inside since they didn't really know how to use magic effectively yet, so it was up to Caleb, Oliver, Luken, and me to make sure no one got to them.

The fact that each of the women was intended to act as some sort of payment for debt their parents held meant that we'd let no one get their hands on them. It would be the end of the women's lives as they knew them.

And I wasn't losing Hazel.

And there was no way anyone was getting through me to touch a hair on Hazel Riley's head.

Oliver, Luken, and I had known each other and worked together long enough that we didn't need to speak to know what the other was thinking. Still, I said the words out loud.

"No one make a move unless he does. He shouldn't be able to see us."

My parents used runes to protect this place. Now, the moment we'd entered, the timer had started, but the protection should've lasted a while. We're talking weeks maybe months, not minutes. Which meant this skinny-ass rat-looking man shouldn't have been able to see us, hear us, or know that the cabin was even here.

If he was a dark witch and tried to cross the boundary, he may as well have licked a lightning bolt.

"Is he one of yours?" I asked, looking at Caleb.

Now, Caleb looked like he belonged to my family. So did Oliver and Luken. All dark hair and dark eyes compared to my medium-blond hair and icy-blue eyes. They looked like my dad, while I...

I swallowed hard.

Turned out, I did look like my biological father. The problem was that I'd just discovered who that was. And it was the man I couldn't wait to kill.

So my dad wasn't my dad, but I was fairly certain

he wasn't the father of any of my friends, either. Mom would've had his balls. Dad claimed me when he found out Mom was pregnant after a night she couldn't remember at the Midsommer Festival. The night the Shadow Coven had drugged and impregnated a group of young women against their wills. Most of those women had disappeared, including Dad's sister.

Mom had been the only one who hadn't.

"Yeah," Caleb told me. "But they're not mine anymore." Helping us meant leaving the Shadow Coven. Though he intended to join us, I thought, in the Light Coven, there hadn't been time for that and we needed to use his dark magic for good. "This area should just look bare to him."

Oliver leaned forward so that he could see Caleb. "How come you can see it?"

That was an excellent question.

"It's the Fae blood you all have me drinking like it's tequila on prom night." He looked back out at the dark witch. "It has to be."

I snorted. Drinking Fae blood couldn't have been all that pleasant. "Maybe we could get it into an amulet or something. So that you don't have to drink it."

He nodded. "Excellent idea."

It was a weird juxtaposition. Each of us was ready to fight, to kill, but we were talking about amulets and Fae blood.

The stringy dark witch walked around the perimeter like he was trying to find a weakness, but he wasn't even supposed to know this was here. Every few steps, he would wince, like he could feel the power coming from the ruins.

"What's he doing?" I muttered.

"He can probably feel something, but the runes should be telling him to run in the opposite direction." He shook his head. "Alvin wasn't our brightest member."

Suddenly, a second man stepped out of the woods. This guy was big, like a goon. His shaved head made him look bigger, I thought. But when it came to magic, size didn't matter.

The door to the cabin opened quietly, as if someone were trying to exit without being caught. I glanced over to see Hazel slipping out, her red hair slightly unkempt as it hung down her back and right away, I shook my head. That woman wasn't the best at doing as she was told.

"What're you doing?" I asked as soon as she'd gotten to me. Since clearly, the men on the outside couldn't hear us, I wasn't as concerned.

"I saw the second guy come out of the woods." She pushed a lock of hair behind her ear and looked up at me with those brilliant, green eyes.

"There're four of us and two of them," I explained. "We're not worried. You can go back inside."

She swallowed hard and shook those curls. "That's not why I came out here. But he..." She took a deep breath. "He's one of the goons who took me from your house."

My muscles tightened and hot rage shot through my veins. "He what?"

"He was one of them. He was at your house. He's the one who ripped the amulet off me."

I turned and, without meaning to, began walking toward the witch in question. Oliver and Luken jumped in front of me, putting their hands on my chest to stop me from going any farther.

"You can't go out there," Luken said. "It doesn't matter how much you want to rip that guy's head off right now. You can't. It'll have to wait."

"Fuck that, Luken."

"You'll just cause more problems," Caleb told me, though I didn't think it was the smartest choice for him to be giving me advice right now. I didn't know him. Didn't trust him. "If you go out there, then they know we're here. That we're hidden. It'll put everyone in danger."

Fuck. I hated knowing that he was right.

"Fine," I spat through clenched teeth, but I didn't make any move to return to where I started.

Caleb knew my weak spot. Hazel. Keeping Hazel safe. Protecting her. That was my priority and I wasn't going to do anything to risk her.

"Why don't you go inside with the women?" Luken slapped my back as Oliver turned me around so I'd walk back to where we'd all been a moment ago. "Get them settled. Nothing's going to happen out here and we'll keep an eye on these two until they leave."

Not exactly what I wanted to do, but they were right. If I didn't get out of here right now, I was liable to go over and rip that witch's head off.

"Let's go," I said as I slid my hand to the small of Hazel's back and led her into the cabin.

Hazel was still wearing the jean shorts and T-shirt she'd been wearing when we'd left my house. There'd been no reason for her to change.

I shut the door behind us to find Nellie and Gia, Hazel's roommates from the camp, though I hadn't learned their last names yet. They stood close together like they were waiting for something to happen.

I really needed to find out what had happened in that camp that had them so skittish.

"Don't worry," I told them and I hoped they'd take some comfort from it. "They can't see us. The runes are working."

"How did you find this place?" Nellie asked as she stepped forward. She had her blonde hair in a ponytail that made her look even younger than she was.

That was right. The women had been upstairs packing some bags when Dad explained everything to me. "This is my parents' place. They bought it a long time ago and I didn't even know they had it. It's just for emergencies and this is one of them." I slid my arm around Hazel's shoulders and pulled her into me. "They'll do anything to protect you three."

"Why?" Gia asked. Her brown pixie cut looked the same as it had when we'd gotten them from the camp. Not a hair out of place after making our quick get away. Probably the benefit of having short hair and her blue eyes were so clear that they rivaled mine. Only mine were icy.

"Because they know that I love her and she cares about you. Not to mention, any time they can work to take down the Shadow Coven, they're going to do it."

"Can I talk to you?" Hazel asked quietly.

Nodding, I led her to the first room I found and assumed this would be ours. After bringing her inside, I shut the door behind us. Alone time with my girl wasn't something I ever got enough of.

"You OK?" I asked.

"Yeah. I'm OK. I just thought we could use a minute."

No kidding. With a sigh, I dropped onto the end of the bed, reached out to grab her hips, and pulled her toward me so that she was standing between my knees. I wanted her close. No, I *needed* her close. Those few days without her had fucked with my head. Well, it was really all of the thoughts about what they could've been doing to her that had fucked me up.

Luckily, none of that happened.

I pressed my forehead against her stomach and wrapped my arms around her waist. Hazel threaded her fingers through my hair, brushing gently.

"Are you OK?" she asked in a hushed tone that told me she didn't want anyone else to hear her. Though I didn't think they'd be able to unless we were loud.

"I'm OK now that you're back."

She shook her head slightly and there was a kind gentleness in her eyes when she tugged on the hair on the back of my head so I'd look up at her. Before she spoke again, she sat on the bed beside me with one leg folded under her so she could face me.

After taking my hand in hers, she said, "I'm not talking about that. You got some life-altering news today. Are you OK?"

Oh. That.

"Yeah, Hazel. I'm fine. Nothing's changed for me. My dad is my dad and I don't care what biology says. All it's done is make me want to wrap my hands around Michael's neck until he chokes."

She swallowed hard. "I can understand that, given what he did to your mom. But I don't think you being murderous is supposed to turn me on."

I snorted. "It's not me being murderous, baby. It's me being protective. You like it."

She shrugged because she couldn't deny it.

Before we'd been forced here, I'd learned that the man who had been the head of our witch coven for decades was really a dark witch who'd been hiding his dark magic from us so that he could funnel light witches over to the dark side. Oh, yeah... he was also the man who'd drugged my mother and gotten her pregnant with me. An event that I'd also just recently found out about.

There was probably a need for some intense therapy in there, but it'd have to wait. Right now, I still had Michael to deal with, the Shadow Coven, Hazel's parents, and probably ten other things that I wasn't even thinking about.

That was the priority. Everything else could wait and if I had my girl with me, I was better for it.

"If you're sure," she said as she nuzzled into my side.

"I'm sure. I've got you. That's what matters."

Gently, I leaned the two of us back so that we were against the mattress. There wasn't ever a time that I didn't want Hazel, but that wasn't why I was doing this. I just wanted her close.

"The girls and I found that there are four bedrooms," she told me. "So we'll have enough if a few don't mind sharing."

After giving her hips a squeeze, I told her, "I don't mind sharing with you."

She snickered but shoved against my chest. A motion that barely moved me. "I figured that. So you and me in one room. Nellie and Gia in another. Luken and Oliver because they're friends, right? Then Caleb in the fourth."

"Sounds like a plan."

After only a moment of the two of us lying there, Luken's and Oliver's voices sounded from the living room. Which meant it was time to return to the group.

As soon as we were out there, Luken told me, "They left."

"While bitching about there being nothing out here," Oliver added.

"Good." That was the best I could think to say.

"Why don't I see what we can make for dinner?" Hazel offered. "I don't know about the rest of you, but I'm starving."

Yeah. We hadn't eaten since breakfast and while it seemed like only minutes had passed since then, it was actually coming around to dinner time. Everyone could use a full belly and a good night's sleep.

This was going to last a while.

Nellie and Gia went to the kitchen with her and when I dropped onto the couch, I could hear the noise of them unpacking the food my mother had sent. At least this place had a solar powered generator like the other one Dad had taken us to. We should be fine for a while.

And the thing was silent as hell.

"So what're we going to do?" Caleb asked. "Sit around here until when?"

"I don't know," I told him, not liking the idea that we weren't being proactive any more than he apparently didn't. "We'll stay here as long as we need to." My eyes met his. "I mean, you can leave whenever you want to, but the women can't. That means I'm here as long as I need to be."

He shook me off. "I'm not leaving. I just want to know what the plan is."

"I think the plan should be to let them have a breather," Luken offered. "We have things we can do during this time, though. We can train the ladies on some things so they won't be helpless should anyone get to them. Caleb and I can see if there's a work-around to the unbinding, but I don't think there is one. If any of us have a phone that could be traced, we need to ditch it. I think ours"—he motioned to me, Oliver, and him—"should be good. What about you?"

Caleb shook his head. "I didn't bring it. That's the first thing they'd check. I dropped it in the woods back at the camp."

"Good," I told him. That was good thinking after all. "What about your dark magic? Are they going to trace it?"

He shrugged. "They can try. I don't have a tracker and we're behind this cloak. I don't think it'll work. I also cast my own spell to hide from them, so we should be covered." He ran a tongue over his bottom lip. "I'm not binding my own shit because you said we might need my dark magic."

"Yeah," Luken agreed. "We might and if they can't track you right now, then you're good."

The four of us talked about how our day was going to go tomorrow since we all knew tonight was going to end early. Before long, Hazel called out that they'd made spaghetti and it was ready.

This might've been our first night here, but I had a hunch that there was going to be a few more.

I'd stay here forever if that was what it took to keep Hazel safe from anyone who wanted to hurt her.

2

———

HAZEL

THERE WAS no place I'd have rather been than in Miller's arms.

If someone would've told me days ago that I'd be all swoony to be in Miller's arms, I would've laughed in the person's face.

Sure, I loved Miller. I'd loved him before I'd been taken, but I'd never really been the kind of woman who basked in the joy of a guy holding her. But he'd folded his big body around me last night, a thick leg over mine, as if he'd wanted to be sure no one would be able to take me away from him.

As if there hadn't been seven layers of protection already there.

He was still asleep when I tried slipping from the

bed. As soon as I moved, his arm tightened around my waist.

"I'm just going to the bathroom," I told him.

He nuzzled his nose into my hair. "I'd rather you stay here."

After snorting, I said, "I think in about three minutes, you won't like that I stayed." Because eventually, my bladder would give out.

"Fine," he said, but it sounded like a sigh as he released me.

Since I'd slept in a tank top and shorts, I didn't see a need to change before hurrying to the restroom. Once I was out, the smell of bacon drew me to the kitchen, where I found Luken and Oliver making breakfast.

"You two can cook?" I asked as I sat down in a chair at the table that would barely fit us all. There were seven of us and I counted six chairs.

Luken glanced over his shoulder. "Had to learn." Then he focused back on what he was doing. "My mom died when I was fifteen. The coven took me in, but they set me up in my own place. There's only so much pizza you can eat."

Open mouth, insert foot. "I'm sorry," I said quietly.

"It's OK, Hazel." He gave me a friendly smile before turning back to the stove. "You didn't know."

Oliver pulled some toast out of the toaster and while that wasn't really cooking, I watched him flip the bacon as well. "And my mother was adamant that I wasn't going to be a burden on my future wife."

A big smile spread across my face. "It sounds like I'd like your mother."

He snorted. "Probably."

Nellie and Gia joined us and they were still in their pajamas so I didn't feel underdressed. But when Miller and Caleb came out, they were dressed in jeans and a T-shirt, just like Oliver and Luken. Was that the hot guy uniform or something?

"Just in time." Luken greeted the two of them with a nod. "Breakfast is ready."

They'd made a metric ton of eggs, probably several pounds of bacon, and at least an entire loaf of bread. Made me wonder who in the hell was going to eat all of this, but then I remembered that the guys ate a lot.

Once everything was on the table, I was reminded that we'd be a chair down. I didn't mind standing, but then Miller dropped into the one closest to me and pulled me onto his lap. I was perched there and at first thought of protesting, but the feel of his large hand on my hip kept me in place.

Then everything was passed around the table, reminding me of those family dinners you saw on TV. Those weren't something I'd ever had. Even when Mom, Dad, and I *had* gathered around the table, it'd been tense and not all that pleasant.

"So, what really went on at the camp?" Oliver asked before shoving a fork full of eggs in his mouth.

We girls glanced at each other, but I decided to take control. After all, he was my boyfriend's friend.

"I mean, they were there longer than I was," I started, then I nibbled on some bacon. "But it wasn't... all that bad."

"What?" Luken furrowed his brows.

Nellie and Gia bothe had their eyes wide as they waited for whatever else I was going to say.

"Yeah, I mean, it wasn't where I wanted to be, but they didn't whip us or fling gruel at us or anything."

Caleb snorted, which got him some questioning looks. "I'm just surprised Hazel isn't saying we flung gruel at her. She told me the food tasted like ass."

The guys chuckled as I rolled my eyes. "I was trying to distract you so that Gia could get into the main office."

"You're distracting enough," he said, but he clearly hadn't thought about how that would sound.

Miller's hand tightened where it lay on my hip as he opened his mouth.

I swooped in before he could say anything. "But it did taste like ass, by the way."

"You were tasting the magic," he told me, which was what I'd expected all along. I assumed that they were doing something to the food. I just didn't know what.

"I was tasting the what?"

"They put a potion in it to make you all... more open to dark magic."

I dropped my fork and it hit the plate with a loud clang. "I knew it. I knew there was something wrong with it. That's why I ate almost nothing. If you knew that, why didn't you tell us?"

"I couldn't," he told me. "You know they spelled me on certain things so that I couldn't tell you unless you already knew."

"I knew," I countered.

He shook his head. "You suspected. You guessed. But you didn't know."

"If that's true, why didn't it work?" Nellie asked the question that I knew at least the three of us were thinking. Though none of us had eaten any more than we'd had to to stay alive.

Caleb shrugged. "I don't know. It should've. But I'm going to guess it's whatever reason I also started questioning everything once Hazel arrived."

"I think most of us can guess why that was," Miller mumbled, but I didn't think that was it.

Caleb being attracted to me, which was what Miller was insinuating, wouldn't have had anything to do with why Nellie, Gia, and our other roommate, Juniper, hadn't been coerced by the magic in the food. For that matter, it wasn't a reason for me not to have been affected.

"Not what I was thinking," he countered. "Since she got there, I started to question everything. Why I dedicated my life to dark magic and the Shadow Coven. I was born into it, sure, and it's almost impossible to leave. But I've wondered if my sudden questioning of everything doesn't have something to with whatever Hazel's special talent is."

On the one hand, he hadn't denied what Miller had said without saying it. On the other, he said I had a special talent. Was it possible that my natural-born talent could help strip away whatever made a person a dark witch? I had no idea. There was still so much to learn.

Miller's jaw was tight when he said, "Well, we won't know until her powers are unbound. What else?"

That was for me. "It was just like you might think it was. Kind of like I'd imagine camp with their schedules and rules, but like they held meetings for us to hear how great the coven is. How we'd get our full powers once we pledged to them. Caleb was like our camp counselor leading us around. Making sure we got where we were going."

Caleb snorted again. That wasn't exactly how it had been, but he'd apparently go with it.

Gia spoke up. "The pressure was insane."

"'Pressure'?" Luken asked her as he munched on some bacon.

"Pressure to commit. They acted like if you didn't, then you'd lose everything. No one would ever see you again or something. I guess that was true for Juniper. If she hadn't taken the vow, she would've lost her little brother."

That was true. They didn't say it, but it was how we all felt.

Juniper wouldn't leave with us when Miller and the guys showed up. She stayed and took the pledge to save her little brother.

Deep down, I hoped that once all of the other

shit was over, we could somehow coax Juniper out of the Shadow Coven. Maybe we could bring her little brother with her because, without him, she wasn't going anywhere.

"Well, that one woman no one did ever hear from again," Nellie added. Then before anyone could ask, she said, "She told them she wasn't a virgin when she got there. Then she was gone."

The group of us got really quiet for a minute.

Luken set his elbows on the table. "How did they get you all to cooperate?"

"Well, none of us had magic," I offered. "I mean, I guess we did a little because we found a weak spot in the back clearing where I tried to send Miller a message."

He ran a hand down the back of my hair. "I got it."

"For Juniper, it was her little brother." Gia pushed her plate away from her and wrapped her arms over her stomach. We were all still sick over Juniper.

"They threatened her little brother?" All of Miller's muscles were tense when he asked. Gia nodded, then his gaze fell heavily on mine. "And with you?"

I shrugged. "You. Your family. Them." I pointed

at Oliver and Luken. "I didn't even know your family, but I didn't want anything to happen to them. That would've been devastating for you. I wasn't going to be the cause of it."

"*That's* why you agreed to cooperate?" Caleb asked.

"What?" Miller snapped.

"Hold on." I put my hand up to calm him before he lost his shit. "I did agree to cooperate, but I never actually intended to. I just thought it was safer for them to think I would until I knew what was going on. You can ask Nellie and Gia." But what I left out was the fact that in the end, if it came to Miller's safety, I would've joined. I'd rather lose him and commit myself to a life I hated than have anything happen to him.

Of course, I hadn't known about the dark Fae at the time. Being someone's battery sounded awful.

It was a tense moment before Miller finally nodded. "I can see that."

"OK." Luken pushed from the table. "We have to get this place shored up. We've got work to do. And I think you three should start or continue learning right away. Your magic might be bound, but that doesn't mean you can't use spells or potions."

"That's a good idea," Oliver added. "Maybe get

dressed first, though." He turned away and I began to wonder if he had a thing for one of the other girls, judging by the way he was avoiding looking directly at either of them. Me, he'd lock eyes with, no problem. But I was already with Miller.

That would be awesome, actually. Luken and Nellie, Oliver and Gia, Caleb and... I didn't know who. Personality-wise, they all matched, but that would've been too perfect. Either way, relationship or not, I wanted them all to be part of the family I was going to have to put together myself because the one I'd been born into sucked so hard.

Nellie, Gia, and I were dressed in shorts and T-shirts, excited to learn and get the cabin ready in any way we could.

"Luken found a way for us to use the Fae blood in an amulet." Oliver shuffled over from the kitchen, where he'd just tossed a towel onto the countertop. "So Caleb doesn't have to drink it every time he wants to pass through. It might last longer, too. We decided that you three are going to work with Luken." He waved a hand in our general direction. "Caleb, Miller, and I are going to fortify the wards. Put up new ones. Whatever we need to do."

It sounded like a good plan to me. None of us knew how to do anything that would help.

The three of them left the cabin, so I took a deep breath and headed over to the table, where Luken began pulling ingredients out of the crate he had sitting on a chair. The windows of the cabin were open, bringing in a fresh breeze. Later, the guys would want the air conditioner on because the heat of the day threatened to become overbearing. Good thing Cooper had the solar-powered generator here too.

It was also incredibly quiet, though the runes would've kept the sound inside anyway.

"So, what do we do first?" I asked, wrapping my hands around the back of a chair. Nellie and Gia were right there beside me.

"First, we're going to go over some basic ingredients," Luken told me. His dark hair was messy, like he hadn't brushed it this morning, but when he flipped it back, I knew that whole vibe was intentional.

He had the look that most women would swoon for.

"With these ingredients, you can make other things too, right?" I asked. "I know I saw Miller use some of them the other morning. They aren't only used for one thing?"

Luken nodded as he picked up a vial. "That's

true. It's about the combination of ingredients. That's what you have to learn what goes with what. What does each thing do? Because once you know what they do, you can combine them into whatever you need. But you'll also know what not to put together. For example..." He held a vial in each of his hands. "If you use the moonrock and mandrake together in anything, no one will find your body."

My eyes widened and I had to assume Gia's and Nellie's did too. "Why would you have them near each other?"

Luken chuckled. "I'm just fucking with you. But there are ingredients that when put together, form toxic gas. If you're not prepared for that, it could get ugly. So you have to learn them. Then once you know, you can experiment and make your own potions as you go."

"'Make your own potions'?" Nellie asked. I was glad to hear that I wasn't the only one who didn't know what he was talking about. She'd grown up knowing she was a witch and didn't know, so I wasn't doing too badly.

"Yeah." He moved the box away and pulled something out of a different bag. It was something long and black. Maybe two inches long on the end of a chain. Kind of reminded me of the amulet that I no longer had. "You can make this shit up as you go once you know what you're doing."

"And today we're making Caleb an amulet?" Gia asked.

"Yup." He pulled the end off the long, black thing. "This is onyx. Its regular powers include protection and strength. We want the Fae blood to be as strong as possible. So we're going to encase the blood in the onyx. Then when Caleb wears it, he should be able to come and go without having to drink the blood each time. Should mean we can stretch it for longer. Which we really fucking need."

"But it'll run out?"

"Yeah." He nodded. "It won't last forever, but we can then refill it."

When he first pulled the crystal out of the bag, I didn't notice that it was hallow with a plugged end. He took the Fae blood and poured a small amount of it into the amulet. The blood sizzled against the cold, black onyx, then the crystal glowed deep red before fading out.

"That means the onyx accepted the blood," he explained. Then he put the cap back on, held his hand over it, and mumbled some words that I couldn't quite hear. "And that will seal it. It's a simple spell. One that can be undone. I left the unbreakable part out of it so that one of us can unseal it when we need to."

"It's that simple?" I asked because honestly, so far with the grounding and now this, witchcraft didn't seem all that hard.

When Luken snorted, I knew I was wrong. "This is. If you consider getting your hands on Fae blood 'simple.' Sure."

Right. It wasn't like there were Fae everywhere. I didn't think.

"Do you have to charge it?" I asked. "Like Miller had to do with my amulet?'

"No. The charge is the blood. It's done." He came around the table with a shit-eating grin on his face. "Now let's go give it to him and have him try it. We'll see if the runes fry his ass."

3

MILLER

I HEARD them coming before I saw them. The women were asking Luken a million questions all at once. Which made me grateful that he was the one who'd found the hallow crystal and had to handle all of them.

Now, I would've done it and loved hearing their happy giggles, but that didn't mean I wanted to be at the center of all their questions.

"Here it is." Luken held the onyx out in front of him by the chain.

"Are we sure this works?" Caleb asked.

"Of course we're not sure it works." I slapped his shoulder. "But you're going to try it out and see."

Caleb's groan had me biting back a laugh. It was

a shit thing. Those runes hurt like hell, or so he'd made clear when he'd walked into it earlier. "Sorry, man. It's the only way we can be sure."

He scowled but took the necklace and pulled it over his head. Then he headed to the boundary nearest us, and took a deep breath before stepping through. He'd have been able to get out either way, so it was coming back through that would be the test.

While he stood there contemplating something, probably all of his life choices that had led him to this point, I noticed Hazel nibbling on the edge of her thumb like she was nervous. The runes wouldn't kill him, so I didn't see the big deal.

Until I realized that this friendship of theirs probably went deeper than I'd allowed myself to think about. Though why, other than the bond they might've formed under stress in the camp, I didn't know. Apparently, that had been enough.

I watched her. Not him. Mostly because I hated that she was worried. We weren't going to do anything to intentionally hurt Caleb. Not when he'd helped get them out of there. But she watched him.

"It worked," he said, which did bring my attention back to him. "Not even a little tingle."

"Good," I called out as I walked over to him. "This means we can stretch the blood much longer."

"How does it feel?" Luken asked him, which I thought was weird. "Does it seem like there will be any way to tell when the blood is low?"

"It's warm," he told Luken. "Like, really warm. Not so hot that I can't wear it, but I'm wondering if it'll cool down when it runs low."

"Yeah. Maybe." Luken considered what Caleb had said for a moment then nodded. "Just keep me advised."

Now it was on to the next thing. The guys and I had already put up extra wards, so that was done. We still had some things to do. Check the battery on the generator to make sure the sun was in fact charging it.

So I said as much.

"Well, the three of us will head back inside to maybe start a list." Hazel's brows furrowed. "If we have paper and a pen. But anyway, get an idea of anything we might need for when your parents come."

"Good idea."

She looped her arms through Nellie's and Gia's arms on either side of her, then turned them toward the cabin.

"You're really gone," Luken said, clapping my back rougher than he needed to.

"So fucking gone." And I didn't care who knew it.

"Have you two known each other long?" Caleb asked and we all knew exactly whom he was talking about.

"High school," Oliver answered, but he was already snickering. "We all went to school together, but Hazel hated him in high school."

"With good reason," Luken added.

I rolled my eyes and shook my head. "We've been over this. I couldn't be with her, so I acted like an asshole. Done."

After their laughter died down, I walked toward the generator. They followed and I was starting to think this whole thing would've been better if I'd just done it on my own.

"What were they really going to do with the women who didn't make the vow?" Luken asked Caleb, who let out a long sigh.

"Nothing good." He ran a hand over the back of his neck while I looked away to check on the generator. "I used to think that they just let them go. Girls or guys. Let them go back to their own coven." His eyes met mine. "Now I know better."

"We should collect some firewood," I told them wanting to ignore what would've been Hazel's fate.

"Firewood?" Oliver asked. "It's summer."

"Yeah, but the cabin has the window air conditioners if we get hot. If it gets cool at night, there's no furnace. We'd have to use the fireplaces."

"That's true. Let's go."

The four of us left the protection of the wards to venture into the woods. We needed to find a downed tree or something that we could take back inside the runes to chop up. We didn't need a ton. It was unlikely we'd use any of it, but I didn't want to get caught in a bind.

Luken and Oliver headed off in another direction leaving me alone with Caleb.

"So you were the counselor?" I asked hoping my voice hid just how on edge I felt.

"For lack of a better definition... yes. I was supposed to get my cabin where they needed to be. I was to look out for them. Make sure they weren't doing anything they weren't. And... get their vow of purity and protect it."

I rolled my eyes. "I hate to tell you again..."

He held up his hand. "I know. I don't really care, but that's what the coven wanted. Pure, untouched young women who would be ripe to help strengthen the coven's numbers."

That wasn't something he'd come up with on his own. That was practiced shit. Which meant it was the coven motto or whatever.

"Looks like you failed on a lot of fronts."

Caleb snorted. "Nah. I knew what they were doing. I just let them."

I reached out and grabbed his arm to bring him to a stop. "*Let* them?"

He shrugged. "Yeah. I knew they were going out to the clearing to see if Hazel could get grounded enough to send a message. I was there. In the woods making sure that no one found them. When they decided to ransack the main office, I made sure no one was there to find them. I protected them like I was supposed to, just not in the *way* I was supposed to."

And for that, I had to be grateful. Which was the only reason the dark witch was here to begin with.

"Listen," he said as I dropped his arm. He took a step closer to me, as if he didn't want anyone else to hear what he was going to say, but there wasn't anyone around to hear it. "You've made some comments that lead me to believe that you think I have a thing for Hazel."

I crossed my arms over my chest. "I do think that."

"You don't have to worry about it."

I snorted. "I know that because I know *her*."

"No." He shook his head. "I meant you don't have to worry about me. Hazel told the others she had a boyfriend right away. They don't know I could hear them, though. Then she told me. It was never a thing." He swallowed hard. "Did I think she's beautiful? Yeah, I did." Couldn't fault him there. My girl was stunning. "Before I knew she was betrothed did I consider that maybe if she joined the Shadow Coven... Yeah, I did, but that was before I knew about you. I may be a lot of things, but I wouldn't try to get with a woman who already has something."

"Does that mean you're waiting in the wings hoping I fuck it all up?"

He shook his head. "No. Hazel and I are friends. Period. I'm not sure I ever really wanted to be more with her outside of the fact that I didn't want some other dark witch staking a claim. Not all of us are great guys."

Now we both chuckled.

If someone would've told me that I'd become friends with a dark witch, I probably would've punched them in the mouth. But here I was in the woods laughing with one.

Life was weird.

Luken and Oliver came back each holding one end of a huge tree. Caleb and I hurried over to help them get it back inside the runes. Then we set out to chop it up and stack the wood by the door. It was backbreaking work that we did without any magic. Sometimes, you wanted the physical exertion of doing it the non-magical way.

This time, we did.

Plus, it was a great way for all of us to get more comfortable with each other.

Around the time we were finishing up, the women came out with lunch. They thought it was a good idea to eat outside. It was a beautiful day. Warm, but not scorching quite yet and there was a picnic table under one of the trees that could easily fit eight people.

Lunch consisted of sandwiches and chips. They brought out a pitcher of lemonade and glasses as well.

At first, we made small talk, but then Gia popped up with an idea that I wasn't going to shoot down. We could potentially be here for a while and it could teeter on boring. Though with the generator, we even had TV.

"We should play Two Truths and a Lie," Gia said after finishing half her sandwich. When the other women groaned, she countered, "Listen, most of us don't know each other very well. It'd be an easy way to combat that. I'll even go first."

"I agree." Hazel's gaze fell directly on me. "I'd love to hear details about everyone." A smile played on her lips as she looked away.

I was fine with her hearing anything there was to hear about me, so I had no worries.

"OK." Gia cleared her throat. "When I was little, I cast a spell that turned my dog into a frog. I once explored an underwater cave. And I thought my parents really loved me." Her voice was so sad on the last one that Hazel slid an arm over her shoulders for comfort.

I think we all knew one of the truths. When thinking about it, I went over the kind of spell that would turn a dog into a frog and there was no way a kid without training could've done that. "You didn't turn your dog into a frog," I said.

She nodded and smiled. "You're right. I didn't."

"Wait." Hazel moved her away so she could see

her. "You explored an underground cave? How did you not drown?"

"Scuba gear, Hazel."

"Oh. Right." Hazel shook her head, like she thought that had been a dumb mistake.

Gia giggled. "Hazel, you're next."

Her face scrunched up, like she had no idea what to say. I'd wait it out, though, because I was really interested in what she was going to say.

"OK." She shifted her weight. "A friend and I once snuck backstage at a Pure Adrenaline concert. I had my first kiss just to prove a stupid boy in high school wrong. And I went skinny-dipping in broad daylight with a boy I thought hated me."

Fuck. I knew one of those was true. Hazel had gone skinny dipping with me when I first showed up to tell her she was a witch, but hearing that she'd thought I'd hated her hurt every single time.

"Hmm..." Nellie tapped her chin like she was thinking. "I can't see you as a Pure Adrenaline fan, so I'm going with that one."

Hazel smiled widely and nodded. "I'm not a fan and I have no friend that would do something like that with me."

"I would," I told her, but the other two didn't sit well with me. Yeah, I'd known what she'd thought

I'd felt in high school, but the other one…. "Who?" I asked.

"David Channing."

Luken groaned. "I knew that fucker was up to no good."

"Even though he promised us he wasn't," Oliver added.

But I pinched my brows together. "And who were you trying to prove wrong?"

Her smile faltered as she answered, "You, of course. Or rather Oliver when he said—"

Oliver held his hand up. "I'm not sure we need to get into specifics."

I glowered at him. "I think we do."

Yeah, it still would've been my fault because I was the one who'd gotten Luken and Oliver on board with being dicks to her and help me keep any of the other guys from making a move just so I wouldn't have to see her with someone else. I'd known she was going to find someone eventually. I'd just wanted it to be after high school.

Did that make me a dick since I'd been out doing whatever the fuck I'd wanted? Yup. Sure did. And sometimes I wished I could go back and change it, but I couldn't.

"Your turn," she said, looking at me.

I sighed. This was her way of changing the conversation I was having with Oliver, but little did she know that I'd have it with him eventually. "Fine." But I had to think about it and suddenly, I knew what I was going to say. "I was a dick to a fantastic girl in high school because I'm an asshole. I got my friends to do shitty things to make sure no other guy got to have her since I couldn't. Yet somehow I still got her to trust me."

After slipping my hands on the table, I pushed up and walked away.

All of those things were true and from the picnic table, I could hear Hazel say that very thing before footsteps chased after me.

"Those are all true, right?" she asked when she was close enough. "That's not how you play the game."

"Don't give a fuck."

"Miller." Her thin hand wrapped around my forearm as much as it could, so I stopped. "What's the matter? This is just a game."

I took a deep breath then blew it out. "Why'd you kiss him to prove me wrong?" Because that was something else I'd apparently taken from her back then. A first kiss for her should've been magical.

Something she'd wanted and anticipated, not a means to a fucking end. "What were you proving?"

Her cheeks pinked up. "I shouldn't have said that."

"Hazel."

"Fine." She flung her arms out then dropped them to her side. "Oliver told me that no guy at the school would come within twenty feet of me, but I knew David Channing had liked me for a while. So I asked him to kiss me. I knew Oliver was saying that because of you, so…"

I ran a hand down my face. Oliver hadn't even lied. No guy *would* come within twenty feet of her. Not publicly, at least, given the fact that the three of us had made sure of it.

"Fuck," I muttered. "I'm sorry."

"I know." Her voice was too gentle and understanding. She should've been angry. "It was a long time ago. I'm not mad about it."

"I am." I wrapped my arms around her waist and pulled her to me. "How was it?" Though the thought of her lips on anyone else's wasn't appealing.

"Wet. Sloppy."

I snorted because that sounded like a first kiss in high school.

"Now, let's get back there. We still have things to do today."

She slipped her hand into mine and pulled me back to the table. I could've resisted. Being much bigger and stronger than her, I could've refused. But there was one thing I knew for sure.

There wasn't a single thing in this world I would refuse Hazel and going back to that table was one of them.

But she was right.

We still had so much to do.

4

HAZEL

AFTER LUNCH, Miller and I stayed out at the picnic table while the others went inside, some saying they wanted to take a shower. I sat across from him as his medium-blond hair fell into his icy-blue eyes while he messed with his phone.

Finally, he said, "The VPN is on. I can call my parents."

The VPN was just in case. None of us knew all of the ways the Shadow Coven might've been trying to find us. Not even Caleb. But neither he nor I would put it past them to use some of the more common human ways to find them.

Miller hit his dad's contact and put the phone on speaker then set it in the middle of the table. It rang twice before Cooper's voice filled the air.

"Finally," he answered.

Miller snorted. "Yeah. Sorry. We had some problems and everyone was beat last night. But we're here. We're safe."

"Good. We've been worried."

Miller's gaze locked with mine. "How are things there?"

At first, his question was met with silence. Then Cooper said, "They've died down. The council, minus Michael, have removed the spell that made it so we can't attack unless provoked. It's for everyone's safety, really. They've got round-the-clock patrols in town. Your mom and I are fine."

Miller let out a breath like he'd been holding it as he waited for the answer. "Good."

"I'm not going to let anything happen to her, Miller. I've been keeping her safe for a long time."

"I know. I—"

"You don't have to explain. Danna is OK too. Actually, she's kind of taken the council over. Everyone's looking to her right now and there's an order on Michael."

I didn't know what that meant, but Miller shook his head, telling me not to ask. He'd just have to explain it to me later.

"Good," Miller told his dad. "Danna's been

working on this a while. She knows what she's doing."

"Yeah. And with her council training, I think she's the best for the job anyway. After all this is over, I won't be surprised if she's voted in as head of the council."

"Yeah. Me, either."

Silence hung between them as I watched Miller's face remain devoid of any emotion. It was like he was trying to look like none of this bothered him, but somehow, I could almost feel his emotions as if they were my own.

Everyone liked to call themselves an empath, even non-magical folks, but more recently, it was like it was true about me. Everyone's emotions were starting to come through as if I could actually feel them.

It was weird as hell. Maybe I was just perceptive.

"What now?" Miller asked when he finally looked away from me. "We can't stay here forever. I don't think the runes are going to work forever."

"They're not." Cooper sighed. "When we put them in place we figured it'd be maybe the three of us for a few days. Now it's what? Seven of you for who-knows-how-long? You're going to have make sure you keep the wards up and Caleb keeps cloaking the place because I don't know how long they'll last. I'm thinking a week if we're lucky."

"And it's not like we can run down to the store to get more angel or demon blood," I said under my breath.

"No," Cooper said, sounding annoyed by the fact that such blood wasn't available in every pharmacy in the world, though I hadn't intended for him to hear me. "We can't. I'm going to see if I can reach out to the one who helped me create the wards in the first place, but that's unlikely. I didn't summon her then and I can't do that now. Not with everything going on."

"I know," Miller told him. Cooper was trying everything to keep us safe while at the same time keeping his own wife safe.

It was a lot to handle and even his frustration washed over me like waves at the beach. One right after the other slapped me again and again.

"All right," Cooper said suddenly. "Let's focus on what we can do now. You all are going to need more provisions. I know your mom sent you with a couple of days' worth of food, but you need more. We're going to get it and head out there. Now that we know you're all safe, we can do this. What do you need?"

"Food, like you said," Miller began.

"More of Miller's clothes. Since he and Caleb are sharing," I offered, knowing that Miller didn't care about Caleb using some of his clothes. "Toiletries because I'm the only one who brought soap."

Miller snorted. "That's true. It won't last long with all of us here and things will get... ripe."

Considering that the guys had been chopping wood that morning, my guess was that they already were getting ripe.

"Got it." Cooper cleared his throat. "Any other... personal items?"

I furrowed my brows because I didn't know what he could've meant, but Miller snorted. "No, Dad. I've got it."

Then they ended the call.

"What was he talking about?" I asked. "Personal items?"

A sly grin spread over Miller's beautiful face as he leaned forward and took my hands between his. "He was talking about condoms. See, he and my mom were stuck together in a cabin for months when she was pregnant with me. He says they didn't have anything to do but talk; however, I think there were plenty of *other things* they did. Things I don't want to think about."

Oh, right. That kind of togetherness could lead

to *things*. My cheeks heated and I hoped that Miller couldn't see it.

"Right."

"So he was asking since, I assume, we're here for a bit. The same situation, only you're not already pregnant and probably shouldn't come out of this in that condition."

I scrunched up my face. "There are other people here."

He chuckled. "Not in our bedroom, there aren't." Then he shrugged. "Plus, there's Luken, Oliver, Caleb, Gia, and Nellie. Who knows what they'll get up to."

"Nellie has a boyfriend." Even if deep down I wanted Nellie and Gia to find a reason to stay in Echo Valley when this was all over.

He shrugged again. "I'm just saying. Hookups happen and Dad doesn't want any of us in a surprising situation."

"No?" I cocked my head to the side. "My parents promised that I'd be a dark witch so that a dark Fae could suck all of my energy over decades to make his magic more powerful. I'd say that's pretty surprising."

He waved his hand in the air, as if that were just a minor detail. "I mean besides that."

In all of this, Miller made me laugh. He acted as if we had nothing to worry about when we had plenty to worry about and I knew, without him telling me, that he was plenty of worried about it. His attitude had to be about me.

He wouldn't want me scared. He wouldn't want me worrying myself to death over this when he was doing enough worrying for the both of us.

At that moment, it was like I finally realized just how serious he was about putting himself between me and any danger that might creep up. The danger being the Shadow Coven and a dark fae. Neither of which I knew much about. I'd have to get more information so that I'd be able to help save myself so that nothing would happen to him.

"I don't want you hurt," I told him quietly. "Not for me."

Miller's face softened as he released my hands and came around the table so that he could straddle the bench beside me. One of his legs stretched out behind my back while the other brushed against my knee. He settled one hand on my back and the other cupped my jaw, turning it so that I was facing him.

"Hazel, they're not going to touch you and I don't care what that means for me."

"I—"

"No," he said, cutting me off. "I love you. I love you more than I thought I could, which was actually a fucking lot. I'm not going to sit by and let anything happen to you."

"I don't want you hurt."

"If I die protecting you, it's worth it."

I hated the sound of that but wasn't going to argue. If it came down to it, just like at the camp, I'd sacrifice myself to keep him and his family safe. The problem was, there was no way any of them would let me.

Miller got a call back from his parents sometime later that they'd be out first thing in the morning. Early so no one would notice them leaving. They'd take a long route, backtracking before coming right for us to make sure they weren't followed.

It was insane to think that these people who I barely knew would go through all of this for me, but then I reminded myself that it wasn't just for me.

It was for Miller too.

We spent the rest of the day getting the cabin cleaned up and put together then had a nice dinner together. This time, I didn't sit on Miller's lap and instead, Luken pulled the rocking chair out from the living room. It was more comfortable for everyone involved.

It wasn't long after dinner before Miller pulled me into our room. Nellie and Gia had already gone into theirs, saying that it'd been a long few days and they both just wanted to chill out alone. Probably they weren't even talking to each other. It was all a lot to process.

At least I had Miller. They didn't have someone here like that, even though they both knew we were all here for each other.

Once our bedroom door was closed, Miller cupped my cheeks then pushed his lips against mine. It was a slow, wet kiss that didn't mask his intentions at all.

"Are you OK?" I asked when the kiss ended.

"I need you," he said quietly. "Need to feel you."

I wrapped my fingers around his wrists as his hands still held my face. "You have me, Miller. And you can take whatever you need to reassure yourself that I'm fine. Because I'm fine. I promise."

"I know." He slid his hands down to my shoulders and ran his nose up my jaw. "I know you're fine. I just need to *feel* that you're fine."

Nodding, I pulled my head back so that I could look him in the eyes. "Like I said. You can take whatever you need."

He ran his tongue over his bottom lip. "Maybe I don't want to take. Maybe I want to give."

It took everything in me not to grin like an absolute fool. Miller had always been a giver. Every single time we'd been together, he'd made sure to take care of me before taking anything for himself. Though I had a sneaking suspicion that the things he did to —*for*—me were for him as well.

Or at least he seemed to really enjoy it.

As he moved me back toward the bed, Miller pulled my shirt off before his mouth crashed against mine again. He was moving so slowly that I wanted to fling my clothing off myself, but if this was what he needed, I wouldn't rush him.

No matter how scared I'd been in the days I was gone, it had to have been worse for him. He didn't know if I was safe. He hadn't even known if I'd been alive. At least I'd known whether or not I'd been in imminent danger.

I'd known that yesterday, the way he'd quickly taken me against the wall when we'd arrived, wasn't going to be enough. He needed more to convince himself that I was here and fine. That none of this had changed anything between us.

For every article of my clothing he removed, I pushed for one of his. It was a slow tit for tat that didn't end until we were both naked and I was lying on my back against the mattress with him hovering above.

Not one part of his body was touching mine as he balanced on his hands and peered down at me.

"You're so fucking beautiful, it hurts," he whispered. And no one had ever made me feel like that was true other than him.

Finally, right when I was about to beg, Miller leaned down and kissed me again. His hot mouth on mine had me melting into the bed.

The man could definitely kiss. He had a talented mouth and an even more talented tongue. I ran my hands up his back, digging in with what little nails I had, making him groan. Just when I was about out of breath, he pulled back and kissed his way down my body. He stopped between my breasts and pressed his body weight against me.

No longer was he balancing on his hands because those hands were cupping my breasts so he could pushed them together as he buried his face between them.

There'd been a time when I'd been self-conscious about the size of my breasts. They weren't small, exactly, but no one would ever call me *volup-*

tuous. But since Miller didn't seem to care about the size, I wasn't going to, either.

He was a wonder for a woman's self-esteem.

Miller leaned back, those icy-blue eyes darkened with desire. He kept the eye contact as he sucked a nipple into his mouth. I groaned and dropped my head back against the pillow. His teeth scraping against the sensitive nub had me wanting to cry out, but I didn't. There were people out there in the other room who didn't need to hear this.

My nipple released from his mouth with a pop before he kissed his way down my stomach, not stopping until he settled between my legs. He pushed my thighs open wide to give himself room. I'd never known there were men who liked to go down on a woman so much until him. Before, in my limited experience, it'd felt like it was an obligatory thing that was done because it was a quick way to get a woman off and he could get to the good part.

But not Miller. He took his time.

He licked me slowly from the bottom to the top, circling my clit quickly before biting into my thigh. I didn't even care if he left a mark.

Then he licked me again. He kept up this slow, torturous pace until the point that I almost couldn't take it. I was on the verge of having an orgasm, but it was like there just wasn't enough to push me over. And it had to be on purpose. I just needed something a little more.

My groan told the entire story. It was the frustration. I loved what he was doing to me, but I was over not coming. I needed...

That. I needed that. Miller pushed two fingers into me and brushed his lips over my clit before sucking it in. It was that little bit of added pressure. When I sighed my enjoyment, he circled with his tongue again, this time not at all softly. On his second turn, my world imploded and I could've sworn I saw stars.

Breathless and even more needy, I pulled at his shoulders until he was back over me and I could kiss him as my hand enclosed over his cock. Miller groaned and dropped his forehead to my shoulder. There wasn't a lot of room for me to maneuver, so I tried to get him to flip over, but I couldn't move his big body and he wasn't doing it, either.

"Why?" I asked, sounding even more breathless than I thought I would have.

"I can't," he said quietly. "If I flip over, you'll put me in your mouth."

"That *is* the plan." I gave him another tug, causing him to close his eyes and squeeze them together for a few seconds before wrapping his much-stronger hand around my wrist and pulling it away.

"I can't let you do that." He sighed. "I want you to, but if I do, this whole thing will be over and I need to be inside you." He kissed me and it was pretty chaste compared to what we were currently doing. "Let me get inside you," he whispered.

I'd told him he could take whatever he needed and this was what he needed, so with a very satisfied, tired grin, I nodded.

He kissed me once more before going to his bag and grabbing a condom. It was over him before he came back to me and I'd expected him to slam into me, driven by a high level of desire.

Instead, he pushed into me slowly. Every glorious inch by glorious inch until he was fully seated. His warm body covered mine and I didn't care if his weight restricted my breathing. I wanted this. Wanted him. Needed him to do what he needed to do.

This time was different than all the others. Miller had moved slowly before, but not like this. It was like with every thrust, he wanted to make sure I knew how he felt. Knew what I meant to him and how awful the days apart had been.

Of course, I already knew, but I sure as hell didn't mind him showing me again and again.

When I was on the verge again, I knew it wouldn't be long and he'd follow right after, but he didn't hurry through his own orgasm, either.

Instead, he pushed those long, languid strokes until I was clawing into his back as my world came undone again with him right behind.

This was different. It had always been love, but this was proof that neither of us ever wanted to be without the other.

5

MILLER

THE SOUNDS from the kitchen were unfamiliar and that was why I bolted out of bed, yanked on the jeans I'd discarded on the floor last night, and headed out there without zipping or buttoning them.

It was unlikely that anyone would get past all of the protections we had on this place, at least no one who wasn't supposed to be here, yet I knew that what I was hearing wasn't one of the guys or Nellie or Gia. And Hazel had still been in my arms. I don't know how I knew it wasn't one of them making the noise, but I knew. Call it my sixth sense.

I stormed out there ready to fight whoever it was, only to find my parents in the kitchen putting food into the refrigerator and cupboards. Stopping short,

I needed the second to take the fight out of my fight-or-flight.

"Good morning," Mom said with a smile when she finally saw me. "Did we wake you? We didn't mean to wake you."

"Uh." I scratched at the back of my head. "I think I might've already been awake and that's how I heard you."

"You might want to take care of that." Dad nodded downward to indicate something on me.

That was when I realized they could see a lot more of me than I would've preferred because I hadn't done up my jeans. So I did. Not having a shirt on was one thing. Having half my cock hanging out was another. No, they couldn't see that, but it was more than I should've been showing.

"I'm glad you guys are here." I went over to them and gave them both a big hug.

When we'd left Echo Valley, I did my best not to show how worried I'd been about my parents. Yes. My priority had been to get Hazel and her friends somewhere safe, but leaving meant that I wouldn't be there to protect my parents.

Protecting the people I love was kind of my thing.

"Yeah, it took a while." Mom pulled out of my

arms and went back to work. She had her strawberry blonde hair pulled back in a bun that made her look so damn young. Too young to have me for sure though that could've been because she was only eighteen when I arrived on the scene. Dad had only been twenty. The fact that I looked nothing like either of them—Dad had dark hair and eyes—never bothered me until I found out he wasn't my biological father. Now I hated it. "Your dad was overly cautious, so we drove around for hours."

"Worked, didn't it?" he countered.

"Yes, Cooper. It worked." She sighed. "No one followed us. Hell, the way we left, I doubt anyone even knows we're gone."

"That was the idea." He then turned to me. "How are things out here?"

"They've been mostly quiet." I dropped into the chair nearest me and glanced at a clock. It was almost ten in the morning, so it wasn't even early, but it seemed everyone else was still asleep. "We had to deal with a couple of things, but the runes held and nothing happened. We're good."

"Excellent." Mom sounded happy and rested. Maybe it was relief over the fact that we were all safe. That was always when Mom was the happiest. When she knew all of the people she loved were OK.

For the most part, that had previously included Dad and me, but also Luken and Oliver because Mom had taken those two under her umbrella as soon as I'd become friends with them. Didn't matter that Oliver had his own mother. Mom still saw him as one of her own.

"We only plan to stay the day," she told me once she'd emptied a bag. "Just enough time to get this place in shape and make sure you're all settled. Do some laundry."

I furrowed my brows. "You know we can do that. You don't need to wait on us."

She scoffed. "Let me take care of you all, please."

It was what she loved to do, so I held my hands up in defeat. She wanted to do it, I wasn't going to stand in her way.

"First, breakfast." Mom turned toward the stove then pulled eggs out of the fridge.

"I can help," that sweet, tired voice said from behind me.

I turned in my seat to see a slightly disheveled, but still beautiful Hazel standing in her pajamas—a shorts and tank top set that she'd gotten when we'd gone to her house—and she was pulling on the hem of the tank top as her feet rubbed against each other. She looked nervous or unsure, but I wanted her comfortable with my family because it was hers now too.

"No need, sweetheart," Mom said before I could. "I love having people to cook for."

"She does," I added as I watched her, then I nodded my head so she'd come closer. Once Hazel was next to me, I slid my arm around her waist and tugged. "When I was growing up, she'd ask strangers in off the street just so she could cook for them."

"I did not." It was an exaggeration, and no, she hadn't.

"Trust me," I assured Hazel after she narrowed her eyes on me. "She was deliriously happy once Luken, Oliver, and I had the teenage-boy appetites kick in."

Mom snorted. "Tried to eat everything I ever brought into the house."

Hazel smiled hearing about us when we'd been younger. Actually, I noticed she did that anytime someone talked about family stuff. The good stuff specifically. I assumed it was because she hadn't had any of that of her own.

"Good morning," I told her. She slid her hand over my shoulders so that her arm rested there. At least she was comfortable with small displays of affection with my parents around.

"Good morning," she said back, then she said the same to my parents.

"Besides," Mom continued while she kept making breakfast for the entire group, "I'm sure the boys will be more than happy to do whatever needs be done."

That was Mom's other thing. She had no problem putting the kids to work and it didn't matter whose kid you were. I swear that she was the only reason Oliver, Luken, or I had any manners. With Luken losing his mom at a pivotal time in his life and Oliver's mom being overwhelmed after his dad died, everything like that had kind of gotten left up to my mom and dad.

At least they'd been ready for the challenge.

"After breakfast, I'm going to get laundry done so that everyone has nice, clean clothes to change into." Mom removed a stack of pancakes from the griddle I hadn't noticed her using.

It was like the smell of breakfast had called everyone from their rooms because suddenly, the kitchen was full of people.

Just how Mom liked it.

Once everything was done, Luken and I got plates and everything down, then we all settled around the table. Now, there weren't enough seats for everyone, so I pushed out of mine so that Hazel could take it despite her protests. Mom would've murdered me with her spatula if I hadn't done it, not to mention, I wanted Hazel to be as comfortable as possible. With the four women seated around the table, we guys didn't want to take any of the open chairs. It was like a battle to prove who had the most manners.

Eventually, Dad took the seat by Mom. After all, he'd been up the longest and had already been working this morning. Then Caleb took a seat and Oliver dropped into the rocking chair from the living room.

Luken and I both stood with a plate—paper which Mom had brought with her—in one hand and a fork in the other.

It was fine. I had no problem eating standing up.

"Is there any news on what was going on in town?" Luken asked after we'd all started eating.

"It was the Shadow Coven," Dad confirmed. "But we knew that. The best guess Danna had was that they thought if they took the council down that we'd be vulnerable." He shook his head. "They're wrong, but they are trying to go through Echo Valley witch house by witch house to see if they can find Caleb and Hazel."

"I bet," Caleb said. When I gave him a questioning look he answered, "They'd want me back pretty badly, given that I know shit they wouldn't want you all to know. They have to realize that I'm with you and working with a light coven is kind of a mortal sin in my world."

"All the more reason for you to convert, right?" Hazel asked.

Caleb nodded, but Luken told her, "It's not that simple. His dark magic might be the thing we need most to fight them. After that, it'll be up to the council. Well... he can convert to light magic without them, but to become part of the coven, he'll have to prove himself and then it's up to them." Luken glanced at Caleb. "If that's what he wants."

All eyes were on Caleb as he mulled over everyone's unspoken question.

Was that what he wanted?

"It's what I want," he finally said, then he shrugged. "I've never been totally comfortable with the Shadow Coven, even if I believed in what they were saying and doing, which I now know was all bullshit. I stayed and believed because it's what I thought my mom would've wanted." He swallowed hard. "Or what they told me my mom would've wanted, but now... you all make me feel more like family than anyone has since my mom died. Even when you're suspicious of me."

"We're not—"

Caleb's snort cut Hazel off. "Some of you are and I understand why. But I'll prove it to everyone that I'm not here to hurt anyone. I can't go back to them, which I wouldn't want to do anyway. I don't really want to be covenless, but I will be rather than going back. Really, I'd just rather stay here, so I'm willing to do whatever it takes."

From what I could tell, he sounded sincere, but again, it'd all be up to the council when this was all over.

We finished breakfast while talking about less heavy things and the room sounded like my mom's dream. She'd never had a big family but had always talked about wanting to be surrounded by friends or family with a million conversations happening at once.

Looked like she'd gotten that. For now.

When breakfast was finished, the women went off to get ready for the day, since they'd all come to the table in their pajamas, while the guys began the cleanup. Mom said she was going to grab any dirty clothes she found to get started. She was going to wash the clothes she'd brought too.

It was, again, just something she could do to feel like she was taking care of us.

"I'll get my dirty clothes, Mrs. Campbell," Caleb said as he went to leave the kitchen.

"Eden. I've told you."

"Right. I just have something I need to get out of the pocket of the jeans before they get washed."

Caleb was only gone a moment when he came back with clothes draped over one arm while he held something else in the other hand.

"Is that a picture?" Mom asked as she went him. Oliver and Luken were doing the dishes and I'd just finished wiping the table down and had intended to help Mom with the laundry.

Mom went over to him and peered at the small square in his hands.

Her eyes widened. "Oh, my... Cooper." Then she glanced up at Caleb and asked, "Can I see that for a moment?"

Caleb's eyebrows pinched together, but he nodded and gave her the photograph.

"Cooper." Her voice took on a watery quality before Dad got to her. He looked at what she was holding then snapped it from her hand.

"Where did you get this? Why do you have it?" Dad's voice sounded angry, like he was about to lose it. I got over to them quickly before anything happened just in case I needed to jump between them.

And I really wanted to know what was in the picture my dad was holding in his hand.

"What?" Caleb sounded confused as hell. Oliver and Luken stopped working and turned.

If these two weren't careful, the entire country was going to hear them if this escalated.

"Where did you get this?" Dad asked again with his teeth clenched together.

"It's a picture of my mom and me," Caleb answered, still confused. "It's the only one I have of her and I keep it with me so I'd appreciate if you'd handle it a little more gently."

Dad staggered back a step but loosened his hold on the fragile item and now I was as confused as he was. When Caleb raised his brows at me, I shook my head. I had no idea what the hell was going on here, either.

"Dad?" I asked, but his face was stony. Mom had pushed herself against his side and he'd wrapped an arm around her shoulders, holding her to him.

This was something important to my dad, but for the life of me, I couldn't figure it out.

"Dad? What's going on?"

"Cooper." Mom nudged Dad gently like she had when she'd encouraged him to tell me that he wasn't my biological father.

Dad cleared his throat, but before he could speak, the ladies came out in a round of giggles that quickly quieted when they saw us, which was refreshing and might've taken the tension down a notch, but it was also far too happy for the amount of tension in the room.

"Why don't we all go outside and check the wards?" Luken suggested. He was a master of knowing when to stay and when to give someone space. He always had been. "We can teach the women how to do that. They have to learn, right?"

I gave him a nod and didn't try to stop Hazel when she passed by to go with him. One, she did need to learn the stuff Luken was talking about, and two, if things went sideways in here, I wanted her a safe distance away. I wished Mom would go, too.

Once they were all out of the cabin, Dad said, "I think we need to sit down."

Which we did. Caleb was on the end of the table with Dad and me on each side and Mom next to Dad with her hand on his arm the way she did when she was keeping him calm.

"What's the problem?" Caleb asked.

"This is your mom?" Dad asked instead of giving him an answer. Caleb nodded and Dad shook his head. "This is my sister, Veronica."

Oh, fuck. The sister who had been taken by the dark coven and whom Dad had never seen again.

"What?" Caleb was clearly even more confused now. "Your sister?"

"My sister was at the same Midsommer celebration that we were at about twenty-one years ago. That was the year that the Shadow Coven drugged and raped a bunch of the young women from our coven and a couple of other covens. It's the night that Eden got pregnant with Miller."

Hearing it again was like a stab to the heart. Telling Caleb wasn't something I'd ever planned to do—or really telling anyone else at all.

"It happened to my sister, too." Dad had a lot of regret in his voice. "Only she disappeared before we could save her. She's the one that made me realize what they were doing and told me I had to get Eden out of Echo Valley."

"I don't think I'm following this." Caleb let his fist fall to the table with a thud.

I swallowed hard and took a breath. This shit was hard to hear. "The Midsommer before I was born," I began to save Mom and Dad from having to tell it all again, "the Shadow Coven came and magically roofied some of the women with, what we think, was the idea to impregnate them and lure them over to the Shadow Coven. Some of the women disappeared once they were pregnant. My dad got my mom out of town to protect her." I took a breath. "It looks like your mom wasn't as lucky."

"*What*?" This time, it was anger coming off Caleb in palpable waves. "You're telling me..."

"Yeah," Dad snapped. "I am. I haven't seen my sister since the day before she disappeared and have never known what happened to her."

"Fuck." Caleb sighed. "I thought Mom was always a member of the dark coven, but hearing that she wasn't actually makes a little more sense. She was never comfortable there. Or so I'm told."

"Tell me what you know." Dad's words came out hard and stilted, but he made it clear that he wasn't going to settle for less than everything.

"She loved me," he said quietly. "She shielded me from things she said I shouldn't have to deal with, but when I was five, she started talking about moving. I thought she just meant houses, but sometimes she'd mentioned moving to Echo Valley. Being so young, I didn't know what she meant."

"She... wanted to come back?" Dad's eyes were

watering and Mom was openly crying. I reached over and took the picture from my dad so I could see her. There she was staring up at me. I'd seen pictures over the years, but in this one, she was holding a maybe four-year-old Caleb in her arms and both had the biggest smiles.

"I think so. Like I said. I was young. But then she dropped me off with a friend and I never saw her again. Michael explained that she had a car accident and died. There was no funeral or anything and I was shipped from house to house until I was fifteen. I don't know a lot about any of it."

Silence hung around us and all of a sudden, I had a cousin who was a dark witch. That wasn't something I ever could've predicted.

Dad's eyes locked with mine and without him saying a word, I knew.

Michael wasn't the only one whom Dad wanted to get his hands on.

He wanted to personally kill every member of the Shadow Coven with his bare hands.

6

HAZEL

"WHAT'S GOING ON IN THERE?" I asked Luken when he went one way and Oliver the other, taking Nellie and Gia with him to show them how to charge the wards. "With Miller's parents and Caleb?"

"I don't know." His dark hair was messy as he ran his hand through it.

"You were in there," I countered.

Luken came to a stop and turned to me. "You'll have to ask Miller. I really don't know. There was something about a picture Caleb had of him and his mom, but that was when I said we should come out here. Some shit doesn't need to be broadcast in front of an audience." He took a deep breath. "They'll tell us if they want us to know."

He was right, of course, but I had this unmatched

desire to know everything that was going on. I'd never wanted to be part of the drama, even in high school, yet I always wanted to know what the drama was. In this case, if it affected Miller, I'd want to know about it anyway.

"He'll tell you," Luken continued before I could come up with a response. "He tells you everything, right?"

"I think so." And I had no reason to believe otherwise. "Mostly, I want to know if I should be in there with him like it was back at the house when he found out Cooper wasn't his dad."

"If he'd wanted you in there, wouldn't he have told you to stay?"

Good point. He hadn't, so here I was. I slapped my hands together and rubbed. "OK. How do you charge these wards? Blood of a virgin? Light of the moon?"

He snorted and started walking again. "No, thank god. Where would we find that in the bright light of the morning?"

I giggled too because at least with tensions running high on multiple fronts, we could still make jokes.

"No, it's a spell, which is specific to each coven—hell, to each person sometimes. It's got to be specific." He came to a stop on the edge of the protected area. "There are general protection spells, of course, but for the most protection, you need to know what you're protecting against. Then you customize the spell to cover that specifically. That way, the magic doesn't have to be on the lookout for just whatever happens along, and it can focus on the one thing. Makes it more powerful." He glanced at me. "Make sense?"

"Kind of." I crossed my arms in front of me. "I'm still freaked out by the fact that you can just make up spells as you go."

He chuckled and took a step toward me. "You can, but it's best to wait until you know what you're doing because one mistake and your best friend is suddenly a toad."

My mouth dropped open. "Did that happen?"

His loud laughter caught me by surprise. "No. Not exactly, but Miller did end up with a toad tongue that he kept flicking out at Oliver and me."

"I really wish someone had gotten it on video. I would love to see it."

He laughed again but shook his head. "We did not. We were so freaked out and doing spells we weren't supposed to be fucking with, so when it happened, we panicked and didn't think to grab a camera." He gave me a big grin. "Sorry."

"I can see how that would happen."

Luken and I continued charging the wards. He explained each step he took and I paid closer attention to this than I had any school subject because this seemed more important. When we got to the last one and were almost meeting up with Oliver and the girls, Luken took a step back.

"Why don't you do this one?"

"Absolutely not," I told him right away. "Are you high? I could fuck this up in so many ways."

He snorted. "I'm not high that I know of and you have to do it eventually. The more you know how to protect yourself, the easier it'll be on Miller, Oliver, and me."

He had a point, but it was one that I didn't like at all.

What if I didn't do the spell right and left a vulnerable opening for the Shadow Coven or the Dark Fae? It would risk everyone, not to mention that my confidence in my abilities was next to zero.

"I'm right here," he told me as if that were supposed to make this all better. "I'm not going to let anything go wrong. You've watched me charge six wards. I'd bet you know the spell better than I do."

I took a deep breath while my heart beat like a drum at rock concert. Hard and fast. So loud that I was sure everyone else could hear it. Instead, Luken just raised an eyebrow at me.

"Are you chicken?"

"Yes." I threw my hands in the air. "Of course I am. I don't know how to do anything."

"That's why you're learning," he countered and he wasn't wrong. That was the whole point of Miller coming to me in the first place.

Well, from his side of it, anyway. From Michael's side, we assumed that he wanted me to fall for Miller so that when I went to the Shadow Coven, Miller would follow. Given that Michael was Miller's biological father, it made sense for him to want Miller there, but I would've been married off to the Dark Fae. What were his plans for Miller when that happened?

I didn't want to think about it.

After swallowing hard, I nodded. My hands shook as I took a step forward and raised them the way I'd seen Luken do. I closed my eyes for a deep breath, feeling the energy from the earth below my feet race through my veins. At least I was good at grounding myself.

The words flowed from my mouth like they were

a nursery rhyme that I knew better than my own name. The further along in the spell I got, the more comfortable I became. The magic flowed through my hands in the form of a blue... I don't know. It wasn't a mist. Wasn't a lightning bolt. But a blue shadow, almost.

And it went directly into the ward hanging from this tree. The talisman glowed a bright blue then flickered like a light going out.

"Is that it?" I turned to Luken, almost breathless with anticipation of the fact that I'd just charged a ward.

"That's it." He put his hand on my shoulder and squeezed. "You did it."

I squealed and threw myself at him. He wrapped his hands around my waist and took a step back so that we didn't fall.

"Thank you," I said against his shoulder.

His arms loosened as Miller's voice startled us both. "Is this something I should be concerned about?"

Luken chuckled. "Maybe she's come to her sens-es." But he let me go all the same."

"I have no sense," I countered. "I'm just excited." I bounced on my toes. "To you guys, my reaction is probably dumb, but I just charged a ward and nothing bad happened."

Miller's playful smile grew and became more genuine. "That's fantastic, baby. And no. It's not stupid. You did magic. It's exciting." But there was something else underneath his words. Something that I didn't think had anything to do with me.

So I stepped over to him and rested my hands on his hips. "What's wrong?"

"Nothing's wrong, exactly, but something surprising happened." Now the whole group was there with us and I wasn't sure if this was something he wanted to share with everyone.

"Do you want to talk privately?" I asked quietly.

He shook his head. "Everyone will need to know either way. Turns out, Caleb is my cousin."

I took one step back in surprise. "What?"

"Yeah." He pulled me back into him. "His mother was my dad's sister. Taken after that fuckin' awful Midsommer. The Shadow Coven kept her until she had the baby, but when he was five, she started talking about moving. We think she was trying to get back home. Anyway, Caleb was told she died in a car accident, though he has no proof that was actually what happened."

Stunned silence filled us all until I found my

words again. "Are you OK? What about your dad? It can't be easy to find out your sister's..." I glanced nervously at Luken.

Oliver and Luken had known this family longer than I had, so in some cases, I would follow their lead. In this one, I needed to make sure Miller was all right with the news.

"I'm fine." He ran his hand up my arm, warming me on an already warm day. "It's weird as hell, sure, and my dad is understandably upset. But he hasn't known what happened to his sister for twenty years. In some ways, this is better."

Luken cleared his throat. "Is your mom going to use psychometry to see what really happened? What about his dad? Does he know who it is?"

Miller shook his head. "If he knows, he hasn't said. He said it was just him and his mom the entire time." He sighed. "Mom's trying to read Caleb right now so that Dad can hear about his sister in those years, but she could see things more clearly if we get our hands on someone who really knows. Someone who was there."

"Michael," Oliver offered. "Even if he's dead by then, she's able to see things. All the more reason for us to find that fucker instead of sitting around here."

"Agreed." Of course Miller would agree, but I didn't like the sound of it one bit.

This cabin with its ward and runes offered us a little bit of normal in a world that, as far as I could tell, was falling apart. We were safe here, for now. We were protected. The idea of walking out of that little slice of heaven wasn't all that appealing to me.

That was when I realized that Miller probably wouldn't let me walk out of it with him. No, it made much more sense for the three guys to go after him themselves, but I didn't think they'd leave us here unprotected.

It was all too much to figure out.

"Come on." Miller nodded toward the cabin then slid my hand into his to pull me along.

I guess it was time to go back inside.

A low hum of conversation met us when we came through the door. We were such a large group at this point that we all scattered around to find places to sit or lean. I ended up at the table between Miller and his mother with Caleb still on the end where he'd been when I'd gone outside and Cooper on the other side of him.

Cooper and Caleb had solemn looks on their faces and given what they'd probably been talking about, I didn't blame them.

Poor Cooper. Sister went missing twenty years ago and now he found out she was dead. It was a lot to deal with.

"What did you see?" Miller asked and I assumed he meant his mother reading Caleb when we were all outside.

"We'll talk about it in a minute," Cooper told him and for some reason, my stomach clenched tightly. It wasn't like I knew what she'd seen but I could tell by the look on his father's face, it wasn't something Miller was going to love.

"Hazel." Eden turned to me with a friendly grin. "How about I look to see if I can find out what your power will be once the binding is removed? That way, the guys can help you practice controlling it before you start using it. Might be easier."

"I like this idea," Miller said from beside me.

"I agree," Caleb said and they were the first words I'd heard him speak in a while. "You'll struggle with it less. In the camp, I tried everything to figure it out, but your parent's binding is solid. Eden should be able to see past it."

It wasn't something I was looking forward to, but sure. Let's do this. "Will you see... everything?"

The corners of her mouth turned up and her head tilted to the side the way people did when they wanted to make someone feel more comfortable. "I could, but no. I try to skip past any... intimate moments that you may not want to share. But I should be clear about this. I will likely feel a lot of what you feel and because I'm searching for something specific and will probably have to go back pretty far, I will see moments of your life with your parents. If that's not something you want, we don't have to do this."

My parents hadn't beaten me. They'd been awful in a lot of ways, but I hadn't been neglected, had barely ever wanted for anything, and had always had the best of whatever I'd needed. That part was embarrassing too.

"We should do it," I told her quietly.

She leaned in and whispered, "You're safe with me, Hazel. Your secrets are safe with me."

I wasn't sure there were secrets that needed protecting, but it was good to know if there were, she wouldn't tell anyone.

Eden reached a hand out, which I took as a signal to give her mine. When I did, she slid her other hand over it and her eyes fluttered closed.

After glancing around nervously, I noticed that Gia and Nellie weren't in the room, so I furrowed my brows and looked at Oliver. He pointed back toward their bedroom. I guessed they didn't want to be here for this.

Eden's head tilted to one side then the other and her face pinched together. She looked like an older person who was trying to read something small. Maybe that was what she was doing. Reading something small.

There wasn't a sound in the room other than my nervous breathing, which I assumed everyone could hear.

Then, as quickly as she'd closed her eyes, she opened them. But she didn't direct her first words at me. Instead, she glanced at Oliver, then Luken, then her son.

"You three should be ashamed of yourselves." Eden shook her head. "You didn't treat this girl right in high school."

The giggle that popped up surprised even me. Of all the things I'd thought she'd see, the way they'd been to me back then hadn't been something I'd considered.

"We did not," Luken agreed. "We've apologized."

Eden scoffed.

"We're protecting her with our lives," Oliver countered. "I don't think we can apologize more."

"It's OK." It took effort to keep the giggling down. "They've made up for it."

It was like she hadn't heard me when she looked at her son. "You're lucky she has a big heart."

"I know." His deep voice was full of regret as he put his hands on my shoulders and squeezed. "But you can yell at us more later. What'd you see about her abilities?"

"Right." Eden snapped her fingers. "Well, the best that I could tell from the binding spell, it's emotion-based. She'll likely be able to feel what others are feeling, like an empath. It would be very important to learn how to block that. It's like with me. Do you think I wanted to touch something and see its whole history my entire life?" She wagged her finger through the air. "No way. So that should be easy enough, but I also think that she'll be able to push emotions on people to some extent. Like calm down a situation by releasing a specific energy. That'll take some work, though."

"I... can feel people's emotions?"

Eden shook her head. "Not entirely right now, but yes. Once you're unbound and you develop the ability, you should. There was something else I couldn't quite see." She turned to face me. "Have you been feeling anything already? Sometimes these powers are so big, they leak out around the binding."

It took a few seconds before I nodded. "Yeah. I think I have been."

"I suspected. I'm going to write some things down for Miller to practice with you. Hell, maybe you'll break the binding before—" She cut herself off.

She was going to say before my parents were killed and we all knew it.

At that news, the guys began chattering about what this might mean, how we might best be able to use if it I could access it early.

But I sat there quietly with Eden until she leaned over. "There was one other thing I did feel while I was looking into your background," she said. I raised an eyebrow and my stomach tightened. "You endured a lot with your parents and that could've made you a much different person than you are."

"I never wanted to be like them," I told her quietly, suddenly glad that the guys weren't paying any attention to us.

"And you're not." She leaned in closer. "I have to thank you for how much you love my son, especially after everything they did. I didn't raise him to act that way but someone to love him as much as I love his father is all I've ever wanted for him."

I swallowed hard and pushed back all of the emotion that now threatened to take over. "You're welcome. But he makes it easy."

She snorted. "He definitely does not."

And that I wasn't going to argue with.

For now, I was going to figure out how to use whatever this ability was to help make sure that my new family was protected.

7

———

MILLER

AFTER MOM WAS DONE with Hazel, Dad nodded his head to the door which was his way of telling me he wanted to talk to me outside. When we got out there, I was surprised to see Caleb right behind him. Dad hadn't asked anyone else to join us. Not that I heard anyway.

"What's going on?" I asked.

Caleb scratched at his chin but looked to my dad.

"I think you should tell him," he said to Caleb. This had to be about whatever my mother saw.

Caleb cleared his throat then shoved his hands into his pockets before pulling them right back out.

"What'd my mom see?" I asked in the hope that it would get him talking. Whatever she saw was either really bad, or really weird by the way the two of them were acting.

He sighed. "She saw my mom. She saw me when I was little and she saw a conversation that my mom had with Michael."

My jaw tightened on it's own. I really hated to hear that fucker's name.

Caleb glanced nervously at Dad then brought his gaze back to me. "Apparently they had a conversation when I was little. Too young to remember." He paused for another breath then he shook his head like he'd decided to rip the Band-Aid off. "Michael is my biological father."

"What?" I snapped quickly without letting it fit in. "You're saying that he assaulted my mom and yours the same night?" Caleb nodded as did dad.

"Apparently. That's what your mom saw anyway."

Then it hit me. If Michael was his father...

"So he's blood related to you but I'm not?" I snapped at Dad which was wrong. It wasn't his fault but all of these emotions were swirling around inside me and I didn't know what to do with them. "So he's my..." Brother. I couldn't bring myself to say it out loud.

Dad set his hands on each of my shoulders as we stood eye to eye. "It doesn't matter if you're blood related to me or not, Miller. You're my son. We've gone over this."

"That was before I knew you still had blood family."

He shook his head. "It doesn't matter." Then he stepped back and took one hand over to Caleb's shoulder. "We're going to figure all of this out once we deal with the Shadow Coven. We'll figure it out as a family. Because that's what we are."

Caleb's eyes were on me when I looked over at him. This man that I barely knew was my half-brother due to us sharing a psychotic witch father but my cousin because he was my dad's sister's kid.

What in mountain inbreeding had happened at that Midsommer festival?

"This is shit," Dad continued, "But Eden and I have to get back. Are we going to be all right here?"

He meant me, most likely. Was I going to be all right? Yeah, I thought I was.

"I'm good, Dad." Shocked by good and we had more important things to worry about right now.

Namely figuring out how to take the Shadow Coven down.

Right then, the door to the cabin opened and Mom stepped out with her arm through Hazel's, the both of the smiling. Clearly Mom hadn't told the others so that was going to be up to Caleb and me. If he even wanted anyone to know.

Hazel dropped her arm so Mom could keep coming toward me but she stayed back.

"She loves you," Mom said as I stood by their car. I'd walked my parents over there, but everyone else had stayed within the safety of the runes.

"I know, Mom. I love her, too."

"I know." She nodded. "But I don't think you could possibly know how much she loves you until you can feel it from her side. Don't fuck this up."

I snorted. "I'll do my best."

Mom wrapped her arms around me tightly then pulled my head down toward her to kiss my fore-head. Dad gave me a big bear hug as well.

"Everything's going to work out," he said before letting me go.

I wasn't as sure about that.

Dad and I were too much alike. The benefit of that was knowing that he didn't want to leave at all. He would've wanted to stay here to put himself between us and any danger that came along, but he couldn't. I'd do the same thing and that was most likely what he was afraid of.

I stood there until they were gone then made the walk back to the cabin. It was only a matter of time before the shit hit the fan again and we'd be fighting for our lives. For now, I'd take the lull in action.

My parents had stayed the day and it was harder for them to leave us than it'd been for them to send us away. It made sense when you thought about it, given that then we'd been running from danger and now we were safe. We'd needed to leave then and now they needed to get back and do their part as members of the coven.

Except when they'd left us this time, it was with the knowledge that my dad's sister was dead and he had a nephew—my half-brother—who had been raised in the Shadow Coven. Even if Caleb was out now, just knowing he was my dad's sister's kid meant he was family and there was shit to handle when this was all over.

Dad wasn't going to let Caleb slip through his fingers again. When this was done, Dad was going to take him on as his own, though Caleb was an adult.

"What're we going to do to pass the time?" Oliver asked once we were done saying goodbye to Mom and Dad.

"There's not much to do," Luken told him. "Maybe we should all just hunker down and watch a movie."

"I vote for that," Gia told us. "I don't know what it is, but I have a gut feeling that things aren't going to remain this calm."

"They're not." I had no reason not to be honest with her. With all of them. "We'll hit the training hard tomorrow. You three need to know some basic self-defense spells before anyone shows up." I sat down on the couch next to Hazel and put my arm around her. "It's going to take a lot of work on your part." I meant all of them, but her specifically.

While I didn't want anything to happen to any of the girls, I wouldn't be able to take it if something happened to Hazel.

"We're ready for it," she promised quietly. I wasn't sure anyone else could hear her.

Once we were all settled around the living room, we let the women decide what we should watch. Thankfully, they landed on a romantic comedy. It was predictable and fun. Almost like we weren't hidden out in a cabin in the middle of nowhere with angel or demon runes protecting us from a dark Fae.

Other than that, it was totally normal.

Tomorrow, we would start some of the most

intense training Oliver, Luken, or I had ever been a part of and it was going to be hard on the women because they were starting basically from scratch.

That was tomorrow's problem.

Before the movie, Caleb gave me a questioning look. I knew exactly what he was asking.

"That's up to you," I told him because it was his mother's story and he should be the one deciding it.

Caleb cleared his throat. "When Eden was reading me, she saw something that I never knew about my parents." The room was so silent that the smallest noise would've startled them. "It was a conversation between my mom and Michael."

Oliver groaned. "That can't be good."

I snorted. "Depends on your perspective." At least it caused Caleb to chuckle.

"The conversation was about the fact that Michael is my biological father," he continued. "It happened when I was really little so she could see it. I was there."

The silence lingered until Hazel broke it. "That means he raped both of your moms? You're..."

"Half-brothers," Caleb finished but I waved my hand in the air.

"Dad's right. We're family no matter what. We're... brothers." It was hard to get out but it was neither of our's fault how we came to be. All we could do was not let it stop us.

Hazel's big green gaze met mine like she was trying to figure out exactly how I felt about this whole thing but truth be told, I didn't even know yet. Not really. But he was my family and that was what I was going to remind myself of.

"It's new information," he told them. "And I'm sure we all have a million questions but neither of us have the answers. I just wanted everyone to be on the same page."

Luken and Oliver were both looking at me like they were trying to figure out how I felt about the whole thing which would help them figure out how they should feel about it. I just shrugged. I didn't have the answers like Caleb had said.

For now, we were going to watch a movie.

After one movie, we watched another. It was a good thing this place was set up the way it was; otherwise, this free time could've gone an entirely different way.

It was late when Gia and Nellie yawned in unison and said they were heading to bed. Hazel didn't look sleepy the way they did, but I wanted some time with her.

Gia was right. Something in the energy said that

things were going to change tomorrow and I wanted this time with my girl.

I had plans that involved her naked and that wasn't going to happen with other people around.

"Time for bed," I said as I pushed to my feet then offered her a hand.

Her brows pinched together as she looked up at me. "You're tired?"

While trying not to smile, I let a big, fake yawn take over, complete with stretching my arms out over my head. "Exhausted. Let's go."

The guys chuckled as I pulled her up and ushered her toward the bedroom. Clearly, they knew what was on my mind and I couldn't have cared less.

There wasn't any illusion that Hazel's parents or the Dark Fae were just going to let her go. My guess was that they were planning how to get her back, though why the Fae was so dead set on her specifically, I didn't know. Other than she was the debt he was owed.

Fuck that.

He could take me before I'd let him have her. I'd convert to dark magic and let him siphon off me to keep her safe. That was the nuclear option, clearly, and not one that I wanted to use. But it was there if I needed it.

"So are you really tired?" she asked once I'd closed the bedroom door.

I snorted. "Not at all."

A smile came to her face as her fingers twisted against each other, almost like she was nervous, but we'd done this so many times that I didn't think there was anything we hadn't covered. No reason to be nervous.

"Something wrong?" I asked as I moved toward her.

"No." Her red hair shook as her head did. "You make me feel... The way you want me makes me... I don't know how to describe it, Miller. It's like you want me all the time—"

"I do." I pushed a hand into her hair and pressed my forehead to hers. "I want you all the time. I'll be at the garage working on some old car and picture you in my head. Then bam. I'm as hard as a rock."

She snorted and sunk her teeth into her bottom lip. "That's what I'm talking about. Sometimes it's still weird to me when you say that kind of thing because for years I was convinced, you'd rather chop off your manhood than let it anywhere near me."

I pinched my eyes closed to calm my anger at myself. I had done a good job, but fuck... if she only knew.

"I know." I finally opened up to see her jade eyes watching me. "Somehow, I'm going to make up for that."

Hazel took a step back, but not out of my reach. "You don't need to," she told me. "I believe everything you've told me about that time and I don't need reassurance about how you feel now. It's just still weird sometimes when I hear it. That's all."

After sliding my hand around the back of her head, I pulled her closer so that I could kiss her. She'd said she didn't need reassurance, but maybe I did. Maybe I needed to be reminded that she knew how I felt.

"That's never happened to me before, Hazel," I told her after bringing our kiss to an end. "I've never wanted someone all the fucking time like this. There's only one explanation for it."

"What's that? That I'm amazing?" A tight-lipped, crooked grin appeared on her face like she was joking, but she was accurate.

"You are fucking amazing, Hazel, but that wasn't what I was going to say." I quickly wet my lips because as soon as I said this to her, I knew I wouldn't be able to stop myself from tasting her lips again. "It's because I love you so fucking much." My hand tightened in her hair. "I've loved you since I was a kid, but somehow, now having you has made me love you so much that it's sometimes hard to breathe."

Hazel looked up at me with all the feelings that I had reflected in her eyes.

She was beautiful, yes. She was amazing, absolutely. But she was mine and I couldn't lose her.

"You have a brother," she said quietly.

Not exactly where I wanted this to go. "I do," I murmured. "But I'd rather talk about that later."

As predicted, my mouth crashed against hers in a demanding, almost-brutal kiss like I was trying to own her, possess her.

I needed her. What was coursing through my body right now was far beyond *want*.

It annoyed me that I had to stop long enough to pull her shirt over her head. When I did, she was already breathless. We got the rest of our clothes off with only minor interruptions and in less time than I thought we ever had before.

Before I could direct her to the scene that had formed in my head, Hazel dropped to her knees in front of me. I wanted to tell her not to because I wasn't sure I'd last if she did, but I didn't have the chance. She wrapped her strong fingers around me and took me into her mouth.

It was everything I could do to keep standing.

When Hazel had first done this, she'd been shy, timid even. Unsure of what to do. Afraid it wasn't going to be good for me, but there wasn't a world that existed where Hazel Reilly putting my cock in her mouth wasn't the best feeling in the world. Or maybe second-best because I was pretty sure being inside her was the absolute best.

I let her work me in as far as she could take me with an encouraging hand holding her hair back in my fist. She wouldn't be able to do this long and when she looked up at me with those green eyes that I was sure had darkened with desire, I was going to unload and I didn't want it to be in her mouth.

I wanted inside her.

So I pulled her back before anything brought this thing to an end and lifted her arms so that she'd stand and I could kiss her again. With her face cupped between my fingers, I moved her back until her legs hit the bed. That was when I had to break the kiss. To make the image in my head come true, I couldn't have my mouth on hers.

Hazel let out a surprised squeak when I spun her around. I pushed her hair over her shoulder so the smooth skin of her back was pressing against my chest. Then I bent her forward and she put her hands on the bed so she wouldn't faceplant. That was exactly what I'd wanted. Then I lifted her right leg up onto the bed and pushed it over as far as it would go.

"Miller." Her breathless voice brought my gaze to hers as she looked over her shoulder at me. "This cannot be an attractive position."

I took a step back so she could watch me take her in. "You'd be wrong."

Then I dropped to my knees and licked the entire length of her. Her groan shot to my balls. With other people in the place, I knew she'd keep her sounds down and that was the only disappointing thing about this. I wanted her in a place where she could let all the sounds of her pleasure go without feeling self-conscious about it.

Here wasn't that, so I'd take what I could get.

Using my thumbs, I opened her more, which made her groan sound more like a moan. Exactly what I wanted. I continued my work until she was coming undone and that was the hardest thing for her to do quietly right now. Not that she was a screamer. She didn't pretend to be in porn with the way she sounded. No. But she was vocal.

And I fucking loved it.

Once all the pleasure had been released from

her body, I quickly grabbed a condom and slid it on before pushing inside her without giving her much of a break.

In this position, I could get deeper than I could in others, so I paced myself. I didn't want to hurt her.

When the leg bearing her weight started to vibrate, I paused and lifted it onto the bed. Then I spread her knees as far as they could go without forcing it. My girl was flexible, though, and she lowered herself so that her chest was pressed into the bed.

Her fingers curled into the blanket when I pushed into her again. I ran my hand lightly down her back then leaned in and kissed her neck, sucking gently but never once stopping plunging into her.

The point of no return was coming quickly, so I pulled out again and rolled her over.

"Climb up the mattress," I told her because when I came, I was going to be able to see her face.

She scurried up the bed and let her knees fall apart.

This time, when I moved inside her, it was at a much more leisurely pace. I didn't want this to end.

But like with all things, even the perfect ones, I couldn't stop the freight train racing down my spine.

I rested both of my hands on the top of her head, creating this little space where it was just the two of us.

That right there was when I found my release.

And nothing had ever felt better.

8

———

HAZEL

WHEN I WOKE in the morning, every muscle in my body protested the way I stretched in the most delicious ways.

Miller had made me use muscles that I didn't realized I had last night and I wasn't mad about it. It felt a lot like the quickie we'd had as soon as we'd gotten to the cabin from the indoctrination camp, only slightly different. The same because like then, it had felt like he'd needed to be with me for his own reasons that had gone far beyond just wanting me.

He'd needed to make sure I'd been OK then. That I hadn't been hurt and one way for him to do that had been sex. For Miller, sex was a lot of things that went beyond searching for pleasure. Or at least it was with me. Sometimes he needed reassurance of... something. Whether it be my safety or the fact that I loved him, I didn't know. And I was still working out all of the meanings behind his actions.

The slight difference was that he'd taken his time last night. It was almost like instead of reassuring himself, he'd been reassuring me that he loved me—which I knew—and that he was going to protect me—also clear.

I'd fallen asleep last night wondering if he could feel what was coming, too, and wanted to be with me that way before more bad things happened.

As I lay there contemplating things that I shouldn't have been worried about right now, something strong pulled at me and I couldn't put my finger on what or why.

All I knew was that I had to get up and go outside. Given that I was still naked, I'd get dressed first.

As I pulled on a pair of shorts and a T-shirt, the pull grew stronger.

I needed to go outside.

Everyone in the cabin was still sleeping, as far as I could tell. At least there was no noise coming from any of the rooms. Because of that, I made my way to the front door as quietly as I could. Given that I had no idea why I was going outside, I didn't really want anyone to join me.

It only took three steps into the sun for my feet and heart to stop.

My parents stood just outside the ring of protection afforded by the wards and the runes.

Slowly, I walked toward them, though they couldn't see me, I didn't think. Not if the runes were holding up.

My understanding was the wards could keep them from entering, but not from seeing me. It was the runes, whose power would eventually fade, that kept them from seeing me.

But they were there and it took everything in me not to scream at them. Berate them for giving up their only child so easily.

For not loving me.

I didn't, though. I stood there, frozen to the ground like an ice sculpture, while all of these feelings swirled inside me mixed with whatever magic was itching to release from my fingertips.

"Hazel?" Miller's voice called from the front door. I didn't look at him. My gaze was locked on the people who had given me life. "What're you...?"

His words stopped mid-sentence when he came to a stop beside me.

"What're they doing here?" He wrapped a hand around my arm and it felt like his instinct to me. Like my parents, who were determined to turn me over to a dark Fae, were standing there, which meant Miller needed to be touching me, ready to yank me away from danger.

My mother looked me right in the eye and my heart stopped.

"Can she... see me?" It was a question for myself, but I'd said it out loud.

"No." I wasn't sure if he was trying to convince me or himself.

"Now how in the fuck did they get here?" That was Luken and now when I glanced beside me, the entire cabin's residents were standing there with me.

No one answered until something Miller's parents had said occurred to me.

"Blood calling blood, right?" I looked up to find Miller's icy-blues eyes staring at me, though they looked a little darker, the way they sometimes did when he was angry or turned on.

Suffice it to say, it wasn't hard to determine it was anger this time.

"Yeah. It must be." His jaw tightened, as did his hand around my bicep. I had to pull my arm loose so that he wouldn't cut off circulation and I didn't think he knew he was doing it.

"They can't get past the runes, right?" Nellie stepped forward and wrapped her arm around mine. Either way, she was standing with me. Gia did the same on the other side, which forced Miller to take a step back.

After sighing, he came around the front of me, which blocked my view of my parents.

"They can't see her or hear her. Or any of us."

"What do they want?" Nellie rolled her eyes. "I mean, we know what they want, but... I guess I don't know what I'm asking."

Miller leaned down so that we were eye to eye. "They're not getting you."

"I know." Because I did. There were six people standing here who would put themselves between my parents and me. Not that I'd let them, but that was a different story. "Is your phone still hidden?" I asked. "The VPN or whatever. I'm not great with technology."

"Yeah. It is." He raised his eyebrow and cocked his head to the side.

"I'm going to call them."

"No." He spoke so immediately that I barely had my sentence finished. "No way."

After shaking loose of my girls, I took a step forward. "Are you seriously telling me that I can't call my parents? Is that what you're doing here?"

Oliver snorted behind me. I knew it was him because Luken chastised him for it. I'd bet my boyfriend's friends were having a great time watching me hold my ground. I wasn't about to obey Miller's every command just because he was the one to say it.

"Phone?" I held my hand out.

Miller groaned and ran a hand over his face, showing that he really didn't like this idea, but I believed that calling them would make them go away.

After pulling it from his back pocket, he reluctantly handed it to me.

"Thank you." I quickly tapped out Mom's number and hit the *speaker* button so we'd all hear what they had to say.

Listen, I might want to do this against Miller's advice, but I wasn't stupid enough not to have him in on the call. He'd keep quiet. Or I thought he would, anyway.

Or maybe he wouldn't.

"Hazel, where are you?" Mom answered while

doing a complete three-sixty spin to see if I'd snuck up on her.

"I'm not telling you that."

"Hazel." Since she didn't know I could see her, I didn't think she'd worry about her actions. Mom took a deep breath and pinched the bridge of her nose. "Hazel, we need to know where you are."

"Yeah, I heard you're looking for me, but see, I have a family that actually loves me"—I glanced at Caleb—"or at least cares enough about me to protect me. I'm not telling you where I am. Where are *you*?"

Mom pulled Dad's arm toward her then put her phone on speaker as well. "We're looking for you. Listen, I know we didn't do this the right way—"

"'The right way'?" I yelled. "Please tell me what *the right way* was to promise me to a dark Fae so he could fucking feed off me for the rest of my life."

Dad's mouth opened like he was about to say something, but again, Mom rested her hand on his arm and he clamped his mouth shut.

"We should've told you. We shouldn't have hidden any of this from you. And we should've figured a way out of the deal with the Fae."

Miller was already shaking his head, but I didn't need him to say what he was thinking.

"There's no way out of a deal with a dark Fae,

Mother. Maybe you shouldn't have promised me in the first place."

"You were never supposed to happen," Dad roared as he became unable to control himself.

"Yeah, well, sorry. I didn't ask to be born."

Mom yanked the phone away from Dad. I'd always suspected that somewhere deep inside her, she'd actually loved me on some level. Maybe not like other moms did, but she was the one who never wanted me to get hurt. Dad couldn't have cared less if you paid him.

"Hazel," she said more gently. "Maybe between that light witch and us, we can figure a way out of this. But we have to have you with us when the Fae comes to collect. We'll talk to him. Get him to take something else instead."

I shook my head, though she wouldn't see it. "Not a chance, Mother. You made the deal. You figure it out, but I'll never go willingly. Now stop trying to find me."

"We can't," my father snapped. "And I never expected you to go willingly because Hazel never does what Hazel doesn't want to do."

"Are you seriously comparing me not wanting to go to your stupid meetings or do the fucking dishes with me not wanting to be a human feedbag for the rest of my life? Your perspective is seriously skewed." He was going to be useless to me, so I turned away from him. With the fact that I thought Mom actually cared about me at least a little, she was the one I'd direct the rest of my call to. "Mom, there is something you can do for me."

"What's that?" Her voice was softer than it had been. It sounded almost resigned, actually. Like she knew I wasn't going to change my mind about this and maybe somewhere deep inside, she didn't want me to.

"Unbind my powers."

Miller's head snapped around in a way that almost looked painful. He'd been staring at my parents and clearly had had no idea this was why I'd wanted to call her. My dad's spine went rigid and he lifted his finger like he was about to give Mom a directive that she wasn't allowed to do that.

"Hazel..."

"Mom." I gripped the phone tightly. "I think somewhere deep down, you love me. Dad doesn't. I know that. He's been cold my whole life, but you... " I swallowed back the emotion that threatened to make me cry. "You, I think cared at least a little. I'm out here unable to protect myself. If you unbind my powers, I can be taught what to do and have a fighting chance."

The silence between us was deafening. The tension on this side of the veil was palpable. I needed her to do this for me. As a single act of love or whatever fucked-up obligation she might've felt toward me.

"I'll do it," she said quietly. My shoulders slumped in relief.

"You will not," Dad snapped, almost taking the phone from her. "I won't do it."

"I didn't ask *you*," I yelled back.

Mom shook her head. "We did a joint spell. I can only undo my half, Hazel. You'll still be bound. Just not as tightly." Dad grabbed her arm roughly making me want to ring his neck.

"I'll take whatever you'll give me." And I hated how vulnerable that made me sound.

Mom nodded and I wiped away a tear. Then she mumbled the spell she needed to and this over-whelming hit of energy shot up from the ground and through my body. I staggered back until someone behind me stopped me from going any farther.

"Thank you," I told her before ending the call.

I swallowed hard because I knew this was likely the last time I'd talk to my parents and given what they'd done to be over the years, I wasn't sad about that. The only thing that brought me any kind of feeling was that I didn't think this was what my mom wanted at all.

When I'd been a kid, she'd been kind and we'd done things together. It wasn't until I'd been older that boundaries had been drawn and my memory reminded me that it had mostly been my father doing the drawing. Mom had gone along with it, sure. But I thought she'd really wanted a child after being told she'd never have one.

"You all right?" Miller asked quietly from beside me.

Nodding, I told him, "Yup. Does being half unbound help at all?"

"It should," Luken answered, so I turned to him. Miller was still watching me, maybe for a reaction. Well, he wasn't going to see one. "Even only half-blocked, you won't be able to access everything, but as Eden said, we can start to work on you controlling when you feel things and when you don't. Shit like that."

"OK." For some reason, I was nodding like an idiot. "Then let's get started after breakfast."

The entire group of us went back into the cabin once my dad dragged my mom away by her arm.

They all needed to go finish getting ready for the day because Nellie told me that they'd all run out there when they'd heard Miller calling my name. While they did that, I'd start breakfast.

"Don't do that again, please." Miller was the only one in the kitchen area with me. Everyone else's doors had closed. Miller too needed to finish getting dressed, but he was here.

"Do what?" As if I didn't know.

"Don't go out to face any of that shit without me," he said. I gave him a pointed look and he raised his hands to show he didn't mean any harm. "It's not a demand. I said *please*. You can do whatever the fuck you think you need to, but I need to be there with you in case shit goes sideways. Even when you fully have your power, Hazel. I want to be anywhere there might be danger for you."

I set the loaf of bread I was holding onto the table and walked into his space. "As much as you don't want me in any kind of danger, do you really think I want *you* in that kind of danger?"

"Hazel." He sighed. "I get it, but I'm a more experienced witch. I should be there."

He had me on that, so I'd give in. "OK. If anything like this happens again, I'll wake you up."

"That's all I'm asking."

"But in my defense, I didn't know what the pull was. Just that I needed to go outside. If I'd known my parents had been out there, I would've woken you."

"I know you didn't know. That's why you need to include me in *everything* until this shit is over."

"Everything, huh?" I snagged the bread off the table to go back to the counter, where I could start cracking eggs.

Miller slid in behind me and wrapped his arms around my waist then kissed the side of my neck. "Yes. Everything. Because we don't know what's going to be dangerous and what isn't."

"Fine. If you insist."

Since I knew he was just trying to keep me safe and me going off on my own could've caused them all more problems, I agreed. But, in the end, if I could do something to make sure that he wasn't in danger, I was going to do it.

It wasn't like I was going to run out and offer myself up to the Dark Fae. Hell no. That sounded terrifying.

But anything else, I'd do.

9
———

MILLER

HAZEL INSISTED on starting breakfast while anyone who needed to finish getting ready for the day did so. But they weren't gone five minutes before an explosion rocked the cabin. Everyone ran back out to the main area as I made my way to the door again.

The boom happened a second time before I even got out the door.

Outside, it was even louder.

Hazel's parents were there again. Only this time, her father was throwing what looked like black smoke balls at our protective dome. The one thing keeping them from her.

"It'll hold, right?" Luken asked as he stood by my side.

"It has to."

But Hazel's father didn't seem to think that would be the case with the way he kept throwing those smoke balls.

"How in the fuck do they know we're in here?" Oliver asked.

"It's so loud," Gia yelled because she would've had to over the noise. It sounded a lot like having a metal pot over your head as someone banged on it with a wooden spoon.

"Shit," Oliver muttered close to me. "It's not going to hold."

I turned to the women. "You three stay behind us."

They interlocked their hands with each other's and all nodded their heads. These fuckers weren't getting to my girl. No matter what.

Oliver twirled his finger as his mouth moved and suddenly, we were all connected by his communication spell. We wouldn't have to yell anything to each other. It was handy to have.

"What's the plan?" Caleb asked.

"To stop them." Because it was the only one I had. "If the runes don't hold."

It was like the fucked-up part of the universe had

heard me because the next ball that hit the dome broke through.

"Fuck," I muttered, waiting to see what that meant.

Her father started pulling at the sides of the dome as if it were a real thing that could be destroyed and it sounded like glass shattering with every move. He pulled piece after piece away until there was a hole big enough for him to see through. He peeked through with a sinister smile.

That was enough for me. I threw spell after spell at the opening. I didn't have to say the words to make it happen. Oliver and Luken joined me. We were throwing whatever we could think of at him, but he kept pulling at the sides, making the hole wider. Then the runes flickered and disappeared. Kind of like lights in a really bad storm.

This was bad. No one should've been able to do that, yet here her parents were confidently throwing counter-spells and attacking us.

Caleb joined us with his dark magic skittering around the edges. Even he wasn't having any luck. It was four against two. We should've been able to take them, but then again, this wasn't normal magic, light or dark, that we were dealing with.

Luken jumped out of the way as a black energy ball sailed over him. If that thing had hit him... I didn't want to think about it. We needed another plan.

"This isn't working," I called out, even though I didn't need to.

The sound of her dad's magic was deafening. I couldn't look back to check on the women; I wanted to send them back into the cabin, but something told me that wasn't the right choice.

We weren't prepared for this.

"Miller!" Hazel called, causing me to turn to find her dragging the other two with her.

I turned back just in time to see one of those dark balls headed right for me.

I braced, waiting for it to hit.

It never did.

Instead, my feet hit the ground, like someone much larger than me had picked me up in a bear hug then dropped me. My knees buckled as Hazel fell backward onto the ground.

The noise of the dark magic had stopped.

I quickly pushed myself to my feet and spun around, trying to figure out where her parents were.

Yet they were nowhere I could see.

Wait, we weren't at the cabin anymore. We were... Well, I didn't know where we were.

The guys groaned as they got to their feet and I hurried over to Hazel to help her off the ground. Luken and Oliver took care of Nellie and Gia.

"What the fuck just happened?" Oliver asked.

"I don't know."

"What'd they do to us?" Luken was next. There were so many questions that I knew we all had. "How in the fuck did we get here?"

Luken, Oliver, and I had done a lot of things in the name of the coven. We'd been in a lot of fights. But never had anyone been able to do this. Whatever "this" was.

One moment we'd been at the cabin. Now we were somewhere else.

"I don't feel so good." Gia was bent over with her hands on her knees, taking long, slow breaths while Nellie rubbed circles over her back.

Caleb pushed his way through to face me. "We need to get out of the street."

He was right. After a quick inventory of what was around us, I saw a sign on the corner. A diner. "Let's head there," I told them. "Maybe a drink will help Gia's stomach."

We walked slowly, all of us on alert the twenty

feet to the diner. When we entered, it was mostly empty and there was a large booth back in the corner. Since there was no sign saying to wait to be seated, we moved to the corner by the window. That way, we could see who was coming and going and I'd break the fucker down if we needed a quick escape.

The sixty-ish-year-old waitress came over to us with huge menus, which we took because that was what you did in a restaurant. She had silver hair and was pleasant enough.

"Could we get water for everyone?" I asked. Poor Gia still looked a little green.

"Sure thing, honey." The woman smiled then shuffled away.

"OK." Luken ran a hand through his hair. "What the fuck just happened? How in the hell did that man get through the runes?"

Hazel groaned and slapped a hand over her face. I pulled her in closer because while she looked fine, this was a lot for all of us. Even the experienced witches.

"What's the matter?" I asked, hoping she knew that I meant beyond whatever fucked-up thing had just happened.

"I'm pretty sure I left the eggs cooking on the burner. The cabin is going to burn down."

I snorted and shook my head then kissed the top of her. "That's the least of our problems right now."

Caleb opened his mouth to speak, but the waitress came back to the table with the waters and asked if we were ready to order.

"Girls, get something to eat. It'll help Gia." Though I had no idea if it would or not.

Hazel leaned into me. "I didn't have any money on me when we..."

"I've got mine. Don't worry about it." And if I didn't have enough cash, I'd spell our way out of it.

We waited for them to order and once the old waitress was gone again, I looked at Caleb because he'd had something to say before.

"That wasn't normal dark magic," he told us quietly, but we were all leaning over the table to hear him. When we'd zapped out of there during the fight, the communication spell of Oliver's had broken.

"What does that mean?" Hazel asked what we were all probably thinking.

"Well, that was some dark Fae bullshit."

"How?" Her parents were witches, not Fae. "How could he be using Fae magic?"

"Well, I've only heard that it's possible, never seen it, but I could feel the darkness coming from his magic and it wasn't ours." He glanced away quickly. "Or theirs. The Shadow Coven. There's, like, a marker on dark magic that we can feel. It helps us know who's one of us and who might be an enemy. It wasn't ours. Theirs."

"How would they get Fae magic?" Hazel asked with a waver in her voice.

At first, Caleb didn't answer her. When he finally did, he said, "They left after you talked to them. If they would've had the magic then, I have no doubt your dad would've used it. But he didn't. Which means, he went and got it."

"Which means the Dark Fae was somewhere lurking nearby," Luken added, which turned my stomach.

The wards didn't work on Fae, light or dark, and had he come to the cabin, I don't know that we would've been able to stop him. I would've died trying, though.

"How did they even know we were there?" Nellie asked what all of us had probably been thinking.

"Has to be the Fae," Luken said. That wasn't much of an explanation but it was the best we had.

"So they went and got an infusion of magic so that they could get to me?" Now her voice almost sounded watery, like she was about to cry. She shook it off and straightened her back. "This is insane. It seems like it'd be easier if I just did what they want."

My jaw clenched and the anger must've radiated off me because Luken and Oliver both sat back quickly. "Don't say shit like that."

"Why? Because it's true?"

"Do you *want* to be some dark Fae's battery supply for the rest of your life?"

The waitress appeared with a plate of fries that the women had ordered and raised her eyebrow. I sighed and told her, "She's an actress."

The woman nodded and left us alone, but I wasn't sure she believed me.

"Do you?" I asked again. "Because we're all out here risking everything to keep that from happening." And it took everything I had in me not to raise my voice here in this diner.

"That's the point," she countered. "You're all risking your lives to keep them from me. Sure, you, Miller, at least get sex out of it, but they"—she flung her hand to indicate the other guys—"get nothing. They shouldn't be doing this."

I winced in disgust while Luken's and Oliver's eyes widened as if they knew she'd just said the wrong thing. "Do you think I'm doing this for sex?"

"No. That's not—"

"Because it kind of sounds like you just said it was." My anger was about to boil over and I needed to keep that in check. "I fucking *love* you, Hazel. If you're going to go off and sacrifice yourself, I'd rather be dead than watch it happen anyway. And they do it because I love you. Which means you're my family. Which means you're *their* family." That included Caleb, too. Especially now that I knew he really was family.

We were half-brothers and while we'd just met, it still meant something. My dad was going to fold him into our family as if he'd always been there because that was what his sister would've wanted and he was my brother. Dad wouldn't turn his back on that.

Hazel's shoulders slumped. "I just don't want any of you hurt and the dark Fae lurking about scares the shit out of me."

"Scares me, too," I admitted. "Not for me, but for you. We'll get this handled, just..."

"Don't run off and do something stupid," Caleb finished for me.

"What he said."

"I won't." The words rushed out of her mouth as if she thought that would help reassure me. "I wouldn't just leave, but I'm telling you I don't want you all hurt."

"And we won't be," I promised, knowing there was no way we could keep that promise. "Now, back to the most important thing right now."

Luken nodded. "And that would be: Where the fuck are we?"

10

HAZEL

NELLIE, Gia, and I nibbled on the delicious, warm fries in front of us. We needed to eat, and so did the guys, but the three of us didn't want to order too much. I had no idea how much cash Miller had in his wallet. There was no using a card because that could be traced, though I began to wonder why we cared at all when my parents could find us freaking anywhere without any of that.

"So, how do we find out where we are?" I asked, even though the guys were speaking in hushed tones that we couldn't hear. "We could just ask, right?"

"We could," Luken told me. "But that seems weird, doesn't it?" When I didn't know what he was talking about he continued. "We came here, but we don't know where we are?"

I shook my head. The waitress appeared to refill our waters right then, which gave me the opportunity.

"Where are we?" I asked. The older waitress furrowed her brows in confusion, illustrating exactly what Luken was talking about. "We were just out driving around, saw this place, and decided to stop. I don't remember seeing any signs." It sounded plausible to me.

"Oh, sweetie. I would think kids your age would all have their phones on them. But you're in Plainwell."

I swallowed at the name I'd never heard before. "And that's in…"

"Michigan, honey. You're in Michigan, about thirty minutes from Grand Rapids."

"Thank you."

At least we hadn't left the state. Once she was gone, I turned to Miller. "Does that help?"

Nodding, he said, "The only issue is, we don't know which side of Grand Rapids. If we're south, we're too far from the cabin to walk and we should probably go back. If it's north, we're still far, but not as far." He turned back to the guys. "Once we're outside, we can look."

"Why should we go back?" I asked. "Did you not see what we just left?"

He nodded. "That's why we'd go back, right? They just saw us leave there. Why would they stay. Plus we at least need to get the potions. We need them."

We finished the fries, paid the bill, then went back outside and down the side road where we'd landed. Miller pulled out his phone and turned it on while the other guys formed a circle around us like they were playing lookout. But they were still very much in this conversation.

"OK." Miller waited as his phone turned on. He'd turned it off after every use for extra protection on being tracked. "No matter where we are, we're going to need some supplies for the walk."

"I'll go." Oliver held up a hand to volunteer. "Caleb can come with me. You know, with the gray moral compass and all of that."

Caleb snorted but shook his head. "I've never stolen before."

A smile played at Oliver's lips. "Come on. Your coven took *whole people*. Your mother included."

Caleb's jaw tensed as his hands formed fists at his side. "That was them. Not me. I've never forced anyone to join our coven and I sure as fuck haven't stolen any. No one has, as far as I know, since..." But he let the words trail off, probably because he knew it wasn't true.

He'd been going to say since that Midsommer celebration. But I'd been stolen. As had Nellie and Gia and all those other women at the camp. He hadn't done it and maybe Caleb didn't know that we were there against our will at first but just because they hadn't gotten us pregnant didn't mean they hadn't taken us against our wills. Now, that still hadn't been Caleb, but it was his former coven.

"Oliver," Miller chastised. "Leave him alone about that shit. But I do think it's a good idea the two of you go. Maybe the combination of light and dark magic will work to your advantage. Luken and I will get the ladies to some cover and figure out how to get back."

Yet not a single person had brought up how we'd gotten here. I knew they were prioritizing things right now, but it had freaked me out and I wanted to know why it'd happened.

"What about how we got here?" I asked, causing Oliver's and Caleb's steps to falter. "Is that not something we're going to talk about?"

Miller came to me and cupped my cheeks. "Of course it is. I'm very interested in what the fuck happened, but being here out in the open and not even knowing where we are isn't safe."

There wasn't an argument for that, so I agreed and let them do their thing.

Luken and Miller led the three of us into the treeline. It wasn't a wooded area, exactly, just an area with some trees. Then he began typing on his phone as Luken scanned the vicinity. I had no idea how long we were there, though Nellie, Gia, and I found a couple of large rocks to sit on. Not the most comfortable, but it was something.

Oliver and Caleb came walking right toward us as if they knew exactly where we were. They each had a backpack over their shoulders and were carrying another one. When they finally got to us, Oliver handed his to Luken and Caleb dropped one at Miller's feet.

"We got everything we could think of," Caleb told them. "Lots of water. These little hydration packets because you can drink that and it's like drinking a bottle of water. Snacks, a first aid kit. They're all packed in the bags."

"How did you pay for it?" I asked them.

"We didn't." Caleb raised an eyebrow, like he was questioning if I was going to challenge it. "We cast a spell so the store owner thinks we did, though."

"That's stealing."

Oliver stepped forward. "And it's how we're going to get back to the cabin in one piece. Remember, this is all for you."

That's the part I hated.

"Knock it off," Miller said with a sigh. "She knows." Then he cleared his throat and for some reason, we all gathered around him. "Luckily, we're on the north side of Grand Rapids. That means we're only about fifteen miles from Echo Valley. If we get there, we can get a ride back to the cabin."

I hated the idea of going back there but trusted Miller and the guys.

"That's like a seven-hour walk," Gia said. "Five if we don't stop and really push it, which I doubt will happen."

"Right." We could all do the math, but there wasn't a lot to be done, I supposed.

Once the guys had their backpacks on and everyone was ready, we headed out. Oh, after a quick stop at the gas station restroom for all of us.

The entire group walked in basic silence for about half an hour, which I thought was a record for us. With a group this size, someone was usually talking. Miller and Caleb walked out front with Nellie, Gia, and me in the middle, and Oliver and Luken bringing up the back. We were following the road for the most part, but not on the road. We were walking pretty far off it, actually.

The sun grew hot as we did our best to keep a quick pace and it left me wishing I had sunscreen. As a ginger, I knew I was going to burn, but given what everyone else was risking for me, I wasn't about to complain.

"Are we there yet?" Oliver called up, causing us to giggle but earning him a scowl from Miller. "No, seriously. We have forever to walk. Are we going to discuss how in the hell we were at the cabin one minute and the next in Plainwell, wherever the fuck that is?"

An imaginary fist took a firm grip on my stomach. Something inside me warned that moving us was my doing.

"We should try to figure it out," Luken mumbled to Miller, causing Miller to sigh and stop walking.

After glancing around, he began to move again and we all just followed him because what else were we going to do? He got us farther into the trees, where he found a place for us to take a rest. Then he yanked his backpack off his back and handed out waters.

The cool liquid felt like heaven going down.

"I don't know what to talk about," he admitted. "Hazel took us from one place to another. Any idea how?" He wasn't talking to me, but everyone was suddenly looking at me, but it was a given that I'd done it. I wished I knew how he figured it out.

Now Miller came over to me and created the illusion that we were alone in these trees. "Tell us what happened."

"I don't know," I told him. "I honestly don't know." He took a step back so that I could see the entire group. "We were at the cabin. I saw what my dad was doing and how you guys were trying to stop him. Then he threw that black ball thing, which he conjured up from nowhere. What even is that? It was headed right for you and I got scared. I wanted to be anywhere but there." I shrugged. "Then we were."

"So you got scared and... what?" Luken crossed his arms over his chest. "Created a portal for us?"

"How did she take all of us with her?" Caleb asked. "It's not like we were all touching or anything like that."

It was like they weren't even talking to me at this point. Still, I wasn't just going to sit there and listen. "I don't know. I had a hold of Gia's hand—"

"I was holding Nellie's at that point," Gia added.

"And I touched Miller," I continued. "That's it. I

don't know what I did or how I did it, but hey, why do we think it was me at all?"

"It had to be you." Luken stepped forward. "Oliver, Miller, and I are very aware of what we can do and can't do. We can't do that." He glanced at Caleb, who only shook his head. "Caleb doesn't seem to be able to do it..."

"I could feel it, Hazel," Miller told me cutting him off. "It was coming from you. I just don't know what it was."

"Or what else you can do," Caleb added as he watched me carefully.

I was about to protest that when a shrill ring took us all off guard. Miller winced as he pulled his phone out of his pocket. "I forgot to turn it off. Damn it." He shook his head as he answered it on speaker. "Dad?"

"Where the hell are you all?" Cooper's voice was full of anger and concern. "Why the hell would you leave the cabin? And what happened to the runes?"

"Calm down. We're fine." Miller took a deep breath then told him about my parents showing up and everything that had happened up until the point that I'd zapped us out of there.

"How did you get away?"

"Hazel... well, she did something. One minute we were there, then we were all in Plainwell."

"Plainwell? How in the hell... Wait, you said Hazel did something?"

"Yep." Silence hung in the air until Miller cleared his throat. "We're walking back now, but it's going to take a while."

"Yeah. So Hazel opened a portal?" Cooper was definitely focused more on that than anything else and who could blame him, really?

"I don't know what she did, Dad. She said she got scared when she saw the black magic headed for me and then we were all gone."

Something brushed over the phone as Cooper spoke to someone who was there with him. Then he was back. "It had to be a portal. That's very rare. When you get back here, your mother can see what she can find out. After reading Hazel the other day, she said that Hazel had the emotions thing, but there was something she couldn't see. Maybe she can now. Maybe her binding is fading. That might mean..."

That my parents were dead, but that wasn't the case. This had happened while my parents had very much been alive and my father had been trying to kill my boyfriend.

"Her mom unbound her part," he told his dad. "We decided to head back to the cabin. Since her parents saw us leave there, they'd probably be looking elsewhere."

"Just get back here," Cooper said. "Or get as close as you can. Eden and I are going to get as many of the wards back up as we can and maybe a couple of new ones because clearly Hazel's dad has some new tricks up his sleeve. We'll make it as safe as we can. Then I'll come get you. I don't think it's going to be long before we have to face the Shadow Coven again."

Miller agreed then ended the call. We all quietly put our waters away and headed out again. We strayed farther into the treeline so no one from the road would see us.

I didn't understand any of this but was anxious for Eden to read me, as Cooper called it.

Because I really wanted to know what the hell this all meant.

11

MILLER

WITH MY PARENTS shoring everything up back at the cabin, I wanted to get Hazel back there even more. It didn't matter that I knew I'd never be able to keep her safe as long as the Shadow Coven was still after her. As long as they were out there, the woman I loved would never be safe.

"Plotting some deaths?" Luken asked from beside me.

I glanced behind me to see if anyone else was listening in, but they all seemed to be in their own little worlds, laughing as if this were just a normal walk in the woods. Was I really the only one so stressed out that he could snap at any moment?

No. The answer to that was no, but for the rest of

them, their hearts weren't in danger. Mine absolutely was.

"Something like that." I kept my eyes forward so that he wouldn't be able to get a read on me.

Between the three of us, we'd always known what the others were thinking or feeling without them having to say it. Maybe that was a witch thing or maybe it was a best friend thing. I didn't know, but it had come in handy on more than one occasion.

"How in the fuck did her dad break through a ward of that power?"

"No idea. The Fae had to have given him something." There was no other answer that made sense and now. Though the safety of the cabin had proven to be an illusion, it was probably the safest place to be right now. At least for a little while. They'd chased us away and wouldn't expect us to go back. "You know this means we're going to have to take watch shifts. Without those ruins, we have to be on high alert."

He nodded and took a breath. "Though it turned out to be stupid to trust them in the first place." He wasn't lying. Ever since Hazel had gotten us out of there, I'd been kicking myself for trusting anything. There had to be somewhere I could take her so that they wouldn't find her. Maybe my parents would have some ideas.

Though that wouldn't really be fair to her in the long run. Tucking her away would make me feel better, but it wouldn't make for a great life for her.

This fucking sucked and now I desperately wanted to talk to my dad to see how in the fuck he'd done it. How he'd just gone to that place with my mother until she'd given birth without losing his ever-loving mind was incomprehensible.

"I mean, they did keep the Shadow Coven fuckers from finding us," I told him. "We just weren't only dealing with the coven."

"True, but now the question is why haven't they come for her." He glanced over his shoulder before continuing. "I mean, we're out here with basically no protection. With enough witches, it'd be easy, right?"

"I don't know." This gigantic knot formed in my stomach. "But I'd like to get back and try to figure it out before they do exactly that."

We walked for who-knew-how-much-longer without seeing another person or a car drive by, which hit me as odd. Sure, this wasn't a main highway or anything, but I would've thought we'd at least see another car. It was at least another hour before the hum of a motor brought me to a stop and caused us to form a circle around the women.

There were more bad things out there than the Shadow Coven, after all.

"Miller," Dad's voice called out, allowing all of us to relax a little.

"Over here," I yelled back.

The slam of a single door preceded the sound of his heavy footsteps trudging through the greenery. I had assumed Dad would call to see where we were but here he was.

"You've made good time," he said when he got to us. "But I've got the truck if you'd rather ride."

"Yeah. That sounds good."

He slapped my back as I passed him.

"Why didn't you call?" I asked as we made our way to the truck.

"No need. Your mother knew where you were already."

So it was either a blood calling blood spell or she somehow used her psychometry.

We wouldn't all fit in the cabin of the truck, so some of us would have to ride in the back. Which was open and probably dangerous to some extent, but given that we were in danger every second, I didn't think this mattered much.

"You should ride up front," I told Hazel when we all got to the truck.

"Nellie and Gia should," she countered. Before I could protest, she continued. "I'm not going to ride up there all comfortable while one of them rides in the back. Besides, I have a suspicion that you'd feel better if I'm back there with you. Am I wrong?"

My jaw tightened. She definitely wasn't wrong, but up with my dad would've been a little safer. When I didn't answer, she nodded.

"That's what I thought." Hazel walked past me to the back of the truck, where my dad had just lowered the tailgate for us to climb in.

When I got to him, he had a satisfied grin on his face. Clearly, he loved it when Hazel gave me a hard time. Most of the time, it reminded me of the way my mom was with my dad. He wanted certain things and she gave him that a lot, but when she decided something, he wasn't changing her mind.

Hazel climbed up first and went all the way to the front before settling with her back against the cab on the truck. After I was sure that Nellie and Gia were inside, and that the other guys were already in the back, I climbed up. Dad shut the gate with a hard push.

I sat down next to Hazel and wrapped her hand

in mine. If nothing else, touching her reminded me that for right now, we were fine.

Dad swung a U-turn to get us headed in the right direction and then we could all relax. Well, relax as much as possible knowing that we were all still in danger.

"So what're we going to do when we get back to the cabin?" Oliver asked. "We can't stay there long."

"You can leave whenever you want to." My gaze locked with his. "Listen, I know you're all putting your lives on hold to be here and I get it if you need to go home. Go. I won't even be mad."

"That's not what I was saying."

Hazel sighed quietly beside me. With the sound of the wind hitting us the way it was, I was surprised that I heard her.

"What?" I asked.

"This is exactly what I didn't want. I don't want you all griping over this shit." She shook her head. "I'm causing so many problems for you all that I—"

"Don't fucking say it. Everyone is here because they want to be."

She raised an eyebrow, likely because of how abrasive that came out, but it was true. Everyone was here because they wanted to be.

"I could try to give her some of my magic." It was

the first thing Caleb had said since we'd gotten in the truck.

"What?" Hazel asked. "How would you even do that?"

"I don't know that I can," he confessed. "I've seen it done before, though because it's dark magic and you're not a dark witch, it would be... unpleasant."

"I've never heard of this." I scoffed. "If this is something that could be done, wouldn't we know about it?"

Caleb shrugged. "I don't know what light covens know. Or if your council would allow you to know it if it is possible. But I've seen it done. I heard the spell. It wouldn't be much, but just enough that she'd be touched by the dark magic and it would make her hard to find."

"Why are you just bringing this up now?" Luken gave Caleb a hard look.

"Like I said, I've never done it before and... it's unpleasant."

"I'll do it." Hazel's response was immediate and showed just how desperate she was to ensure that none of us got hurt because of her. "I don't care how unpleasant it is. I'll do it. Can we do it right now?"

Caleb's chuckle brought back a moment of levity

in this entire situation. "No. I'm not doing it on a moving truck, but when we get back to the cabin."

"What do you have to do?" There was no point in hiding my suspicion. Caleb told me that he'd never wanted Hazel that way, but the way I saw her, I didn't understand how anyone wouldn't. And he had been the one to say that he'd thought once she was a dark witch, they could be together. This was before he knew she'd been betrothed to a Dark Fae and he'd meant it as a way to keep her safe, but fuck. How was I supposed to ignore that?

"Not much," was all he told me. "But it'll be uncomfortable."

"They won't be able to find her?" Luken asked, though that was the probably the question on all of our minds.

"They will. It'll just be hard for them to see her. It'll buy us time, that's all. Which is why I didn't suggest it as long as you had the angel wards."

"I'll do it." Hazel looked right at me. "We'll do it as soon as we get back to the cabin."

It was only another fifteen minutes before Dad's truck pulled up to the same spot where my car sat in the woods. He threw out a rudimentary cloaking spell so anyone who came along wouldn't wonder why there were a few cars in the middle of the woods and go looking for the owners. Then we made the rest of the way on foot.

Mom was standing just outside the cabin door when we broke through the trees. Her face was tense with worry that only softened once she'd counted us all up. When I got to her she wrapped her arms around me the same way she had since I was a little kid.

"You're all OK?" she asked.

"We are."

Finally, I was able to pull back and take Hazel's hand in mine again.

"How did Caleb get through the wards without drinking the Fae blood?" Mom asked. "We used some of the blood in the wards this time."

"Luken found a way around it." He pulled the onyx prism out of his shirt. "As long as I have this on, I should be good."

She nodded her head absently before turning to Hazel. Mom took a breath and smiled. "I hear we have a new power."

"I guess so," Hazel said. "My mom unbound her part of the spell that's keeping my magic away from me. I don't know how I did it."

Mom cupped her face. "Why don't we find out what's going on?"

Hazel blinked a whole bunch of times, showing just how nervous she was for this to happen. "OK."

Mom glanced at me. "You're going to have to let her go or I'll end up seeing things neither of us want me to see."

Oh. Right. I dropped Hazel's hand and took a step back so that I couldn't interfere with what Mom had to do. Everyone else stood around watching with as much anticipation as I had. Dad clapped me on the back again. Of anyone, he was the one who could at least somewhat understand what I was feeling.

Mom closed her eyes, the interior corners of her eyebrows pulling together the way they always did when she was focused on something. The expression on her face was one of stern concentration, but Mom had described it as watching a movie and her face changed based on what she was seeing. For example, I knew when she was surprised by something because her eyebrows shot up and her lips parted.

I'd gotten very good at reading her myself over the years.

Finally, she opened her eyes and said, "Maybe we should go sit down."

"Should Caleb transfer his magic to me first?"

Hazel looked up at me with big, jade eyes, as if I had the answer to anything.

In this case, maybe I did. But normally, I was making this shit up as I went along.

"Should he what now?" Dad wrapped his arms around his chest.

Gia piped up. "Before anyone does anything, Nellie and I are going to go inside and sit down. Our feet hurt and we have to pee."

There was a round of chuckles as the two women headed off into the cabin.

Once they were inside, Dad repeated, "What's Caleb doing?"

"He's going to transfer some of his dark magic to Hazel. It'll help hide her from the Shadow Coven, he says."

"Yeah," Caleb agreed. "It won't be perfect, but it'll help."

Dad rubbed the back of his head. "I don't think that's a great idea."

"It's not," I agreed. "But I'll do anything to keep Hazel safe."

She did that little sigh again. It was like the fact that I'd give up my life if it meant she was safe was annoying her. I'd have to deal with that later.

"What do you have to do?" Dad asked.

"Just touch her." Caleb walked in front of me until he was almost toe to toe with the woman I loved. "Everyone else will want to stand back. Unless you want to catch a little dark magic."

All of us took huge steps back like he'd instructed, though I stayed a little closer. It killed me that we were trusting Caleb with Hazel this way, but she'd already decided and it wasn't my place to tell her she couldn't do it.

Caleb's hands came to a rest on Hazel's shoulders then slid down her arms until he had both of her hands in his. Then he wet his lips. His eyes darkened and he began to speak... Latin, I thought. It wasn't English, so I didn't understand it and I thought Latin spells had gone out of style a long-ass time ago.

As he spoke, Hazel's breaths came faster. Her face pinched together like she was in pain and her eyes filled with tears. I was about to take a step forward when Luken put his hand on my chest to stop me.

"She wanted to do this," he whispered and he was right.

But fuck, it was hard watching her in any level of discomfort.

Tears streamed down her face right before her

knees buckled, but Caleb kept a hold on her. She cried out right before he let her go.

I descended and scooped Hazel up in my arms and held her as she put herself back together.

"What the fuck was that?" I asked with so much anger that I was worried about myself. Worried I might extend my arm so that my fist met Caleb's jaw.

Caleb's face remained neutral but he shrugged. "I said it'd be uncomfortable."

"That was more than *uncomfortable*," I bit back.

"I'm OK," Hazel's sweet voice assured us. "I'm OK. It just... burned."

Oliver snorted. "Oh, man, Miller. Caleb gave your girl something that burns."

Hazel broke out in a laugh as she wiped the tears from her eyes. "That's so gross."

"Fuck off," I snapped at one of my best friends. "He didn't say it'd hurt her."

"I'm fine." Hazel grabbed the sides of my face to force me to look at her. "I'm fine. Really. It hurt. Yes. But it's gone now."

I'd have to push back my feelings on this because there wasn't anything I could do right now.

"Did anyone bother to ask what happens to the dark magic once Hazel commits to the light?" Mom's voice brought us all back to focus.

Fuck. I hadn't. Neither had anyone else.

"Don't worry," Caleb assured us. "It's temporary. If we're here too long, I'll have to do it again to keep her hidden because it wears off if you're not a dark witch."

Well, at least there was that.

"Good to know." Mom came back over so that she was face to face with Hazel, like they were the only two people out there. "Now maybe we should go inside so you can sit down. It's been a long day and it's about to get longer."

Those jade beauties that I could get lost in widened. "Why?"

Mom cocked her head to the side. "Because you're about to find out that you're not a full witch. That what you are is something entirely different."

Well, fuck me.

HAZEL

I WAS SOMETHING ELSE. What the hell could that be?

My entire body tensed as Eden led me into the cabin. It'd already been an intense day and I wasn't sure how much more I could take. Miller rubbed a calming circle over my back, but his anxiety over what his mother had said flowed off him and right into me.

After all, last time we'd talked, she'd said I could feel people's emotions, so this shouldn't have surprised me. But the weight of other people's feelings threatened to crush me. Luckily so far, it was mostly only Miller I felt, with tiny ripples from the others.

"What's going on, Mom?" Miller asked after we'd all gotten settled at the table in the kitchen.

Eden sat in the closest chair and I took the one diagonal from it. Cooper dropped into the spot across from me and closest to his wife while Miller stood behind me with his hands gripping the chair so tightly that I worried the wood would splinter. The other three also sat at the table with us. I couldn't blame them. This affected them too, given that they'd made the decision to protect me.

"Well, first of all, tomorrow, we're going to work on you blocking other people's emotions," she said to me as if Miller hadn't asked a question. "It's a lot like what I do. When I first developed my psychometry, I saw everything every time I touched anything. It was so bad that I wore gloves for a while. Then a friend of mine, his sister, and both of our parents worked diligently with me and now I only read things when I choose to." She glanced over at Cooper.

He was the friend who'd helped her. Which meant Caleb's mom had been the sister. My heart sunk and without thinking, I looked at him to see if this affected him. It had to. He'd already said he didn't know much about his mother.

"Story for another time," Mom said. To Caleb, she added, "And when this is all done, we'll tell you everything you want to know about your mother. Everything we know anyway. Won't we, Cooper?"

"Of course," he said immediately.

"Now," Eden continued, "let's get back to this. When I read you, I went backward because I've had this feeling that there was a reason the Dark Fae wanted you specifically." She shook her head. "Not that they wouldn't take any witch, I suppose. But there had to be something, right?"

"Eden and I have talked about this a lot." Cooper leaned his elbows on the table with his hands in the air just under his chin. "They could've gone to anyone. Why your parents? Certainly, they weren't the only dark witches looking to cut a deal."

"I wouldn't be any help." Caleb cleared his throat. "I would've been too young to understand anything I heard in the coven."

"Exactly."

"Anyway, I looked back." Eden leaned in and ran her hand down my arm in a way that was probably supposed to be comforting. The more comforting she was, the worse I knew the news was going to be. "I saw how awful your parents were to you, though I've seen that before. So I went back even further." She quickly wet her lips. "The Fae sought out your parents. They didn't go to him. He wanted you. Or well, any female offspring. He wouldn't have known it was going to be you specifically."

"Why?" My voice wavered, more out of fear of what she was going to say than anything else.

"Because your mother still carried a small amount of angel blood in her. From an ancestor thousands of years ago. It's very rare."

I furrowed my brows because none of this made any sense. "So you're saying I'm part angel?"

Eden shrugged. "A very small amount. You could have a single drop and you'd still be part angel. Their blood is very powerful. It gets less with each generation, but for some reason, it's hanging on through her line. Her family wasn't always dark, or maybe they were. I can't see that."

"But why would that make him want me? Or whatever female child my parents produced? Why not just take my mom. She'd have the blood." Because that still didn't make sense and I was going to ignore the fact that Miller hadn't made a sound. Maybe he already knew what it meant.

"Well, it's very powerful. You saw what angel blood did for the runes we had here. And he wouldn't want your mother because she wasn't a virgin at that time. She was already married. He wanted his angel blood to be pure."

Immediately I decided to by pass the purity part of this equation. I wasn't a virgin when they took me, though the Fae wouldn't have known that and I was tired of talking about something so intimate with the entire group. "Does that mean that my blood could reset the rune?"

She shook her head sadly. "No. You're not full angel. It has to be for the runes."

I wasn't sure what to say to this and that was because I didn't know the implications. Angel. And here I'd thought being a witch was the weirdest thing that would ever happen to me.

Miller finally spoke. "Why would that make him want her?"

Eden swallowed hard. "Because it makes her magic stronger. It's the reason the potion in the food in the camp didn't work on her and why she wasn't falling for any of the brainwashing. It's added protection for her, but if the Fae had gotten a hold of a pure, untouched angel-witch hybrid whom he could personally corrupt... Her magic just had to be dark and he'd be able to feed off her for decades before her battery ran dry."

"That's why he wanted me to be a virgin? For my blood to be pure?" The mere thought of which made my skin crawl. "And does that mean that everyone whose parents had a deal with a Fae is part angel?" I glanced at Nellie and Gia as they listened very closely to what we were saying.

"Yes to the first part. I'd have to read them to know the second," Eden said sadly. "If he was the one to *corrupt* you after you were bound to him and had pledged to dark magic... he would've been more powerful than almost anything."

"So me not being a virgin would've stopped him?" So much for not talking about my virginity to my boyfriend's parents and his best friends.

As she nodded, she wet her lips again, which prompted Cooper to hop up and get her a glass of water. "If he wasn't the one to do it, the connection wouldn't have been there, but no, it wouldn't have stopped him if he had gotten a hold of you. It's why now, he probably knows that you're not but is still after you. He's not pursuing you now because of your parent's debt. That could be repaid in other ways."

"Nothing to do with the debt?" Luken asked as she took a long drink from the glass Cooper had set in front of her.

"Well, not nothing. Fae don't like to be taken advantage of."

"I'm so confused," I said with a sigh as I fell back

against the chair onto Miller's fingers. He pulled them back then rested his hands on my shoulders instead.

He leaned down to press his lips against the top of my head. It wasn't a kiss, exactly, but he was there. "It's a lot. But if I'm understanding correctly, you being a virgin and a dark witch would've just made you more powerful for him to draw off. You not being those things doesn't mean he can't still siphon your power. It just won't be as big of a draw. Which means we still need to keep you away from him for more than my own selfish reasons."

"That's exactly it," Cooper agreed. "So we need a new plan."

"There's nowhere we can go that they won't find her," Caleb countered. "So whatever the plan it has to be more than just hiding her the way we have been. Giving her a bit of my magic just delays things."

Now I thought I might throw up.

What Caleb had said was what we'd all already known, but hearing it out loud turned my stomach. It made me scared. Not for myself, but for this group that had become my family. My only family since I'd never go back to the one I'd been born into.

The fact that all of them acted as if protecting me

with their lives was worth it and they did so without hesitation was something I'd never understand. Miller... maybe. But the rest of them?

"So what do we do, then?" I asked. "I can't hide. I can't fight an entire dark coven or a dark Fae on my own. What do we do so that none of you get hurt?"

Eden gave me such a reassuring mom-smile that my heart squeezed.

"One of us getting hurt isn't the issue. I can say with certainty that any one of us would lay down our lives to protect you and we'd do so willingly."

A tear ran down my cheek, though I hadn't realized that my eyes had filled. "Yeah, but why?"

She cocked her head to the side. "My son loves you, Hazel. Which means I love you and I'll do anything to protect what he loves. It's the same for Cooper."

"And I never mind a fight with dark witches," Oliver added, causing the guys to chuckle.

"If you go down, Hazel," Luken said once the laughter had died out, "that means Miller already has and I'm not looking to lose one of my best friends. I'd do this for anyone the Shadow Coven was after, but you're family, which makes you more important."

I was family.

They'd taken me in and made me theirs because Miller loved me.

This was something I'd never be able to repay them for.

I blew out a slow breath as the emotion of the day wore on me.

"Now." Eden slapped her hand down on the table. "You've all had a long day. I'm going to make some dinner before we leave to get you all fed."

She pushed to her feet, but there was still one more thing that hadn't been discussed. "Wait." I reached out and grabbed her wrist. "How does all that explain that I somehow zapped all of us to another location?"

"Oh, right." She snapped the fingers on her other hand. "That's your mom's power. When she unbound you, she transferred her power to yours. Did it hurt when she unbound you?" Eden asked. I nodded. "It shouldn't have. It wasn't the unbinding. It was the transfer. She wanted you to be able to get out when you needed to."

Which meant that my mom cared at least a little about me. It didn't make up for all the other stuff, but it was a consolation. After letting go of Eden's hand, I turned to Miller.

He smiled, like we hadn't learned everything we

just had. "Looks like we have something else for you to practice. We'll start tomorrow."

When dinner was done, I went to bring Nellie and Gia out, but first I filled them in on everything I'd learned. Apparently, I was a hybrid, and one day this was all going to truly settle in and I was probably going to lose it.

That day wasn't today, though. It couldn't be. We had bigger things to worry about.

After cleaning up that night, Eden and Cooper headed back to Echo Valley. If anyone was watching them, they'd notice if they'd been gone too long, so they left. Though I wished they'd stayed. I would've slept on the floor.

Having them there made me feel... I don't know. Safer, maybe.

As Miller and I climbed into bed, the exhaustion of the day took over. I was going to be asleep before my head hit the pillow or very soon after.

"Are you all right?" he asked quietly in the darkness of the room.

"I am right now, but I think eventually, it's all going to hit and I'm going to be a mess. Sorry about that."

His low chuckle shook me. He'd wrapped his

arms around me as soon as I'd climbed in and pulled me to him. "I'm good with messes."

"Yeah. It seems you are because my life is already a huge one. Apparently, I'm an angel."

Again, he laughed, though this one was louder. "Maybe I should start calling you 'Angel.'"

I slapped his bare chest. "You better not. 'Hazel' will do just fine."

"Just know that when I say Hazel, I'm really thinking Angel," he whispered. I shook my head, which he would feel against his shoulder. "What else is bothering you? It's not just your new powers, is it?"

It took a moment to organize my thoughts before I could answer him. "Not exactly, but if I'm only half-unbound, then what's going to happen when I'm fully unbound? What else is going to come through?"

Miller traced faint lines up my arm and then back down. It tickled in the best way. "I don't know." At least it was an honest answer. "It could be nothing. It could be a lot of things, but whatever it is or isn't, I'll help you figure it out. You're going to be awesome at all of this."

"How come you don't have special talents like this? If the zapping came from my mom it's a witch power, right? You're a witch. Why can't you zap us out of here?" The angel blood just made her more powerful.

"I do," he answered, which had me pushing myself up to look down at him. The only light in the room was the moonlight shining around the closed curtains.

"What?"

"I have special talents. Not zapping us somewhere else or whatever and more than just being able to make you come quickly. They're just not things that have been helpful yet. Or maybe they have been helpful. Practice isn't the only reason I'm so good at spells."

"You're showing me one day," I told him while ignoring the comment about making me come quickly. That was a magical talent, but not a witch one...

I didn't think.

Even though the day had been exhausting, I lay there while Miller's breathing evened out, thinking about how this all might end and if there was a way to end it quicker so that everyone could get back to their lives.

A way that didn't include me giving myself over to a Dark Fae.

13

MILLER

THE AIR around us had changed.

We'd once thought this cabin the safest place to be and, for now, it probably still was, but that safety was a lot less than we'd originally planned for it to be. The only option we had left was to prepare for the fight that we knew was coming. Right now, they couldn't find her and wouldn't be looking at the cabin but that wasn't going to last long. At least being here meant we could plan for when they showed up. We knew everything around us.

We had less of a chance to win than I would've liked, but we wouldn't go down without a fight.

When I came out of our room, Hazel was the first person I searched for. Yet, even with everyone else in the main living area or the kitchen, she wasn't there.

"Where's Hazel?" I asked no one in particular.

"She was just here," Oliver told me.

No one else knew where she was, which had something ominous forming in the pit of my stomach. It was like my default setting was now worrying about her and the fact that I couldn't see her had an imaginary fist tightening my heart.

This was probably something I should see a therapist about at some point if it didn't go away once this shit with the Shadow Coven was over, but for now, I needed to know where she was.

I stomped to the door and flung it open then stepped out into the bright sunlight to scan our surroundings.

She shouldn't have been out here alone in the first place, but there was no way she'd step out of the wards, right?

Wrong. She wasn't anywhere I could see her.

"Hazel!" I called out with the newly unlocked fear that she'd zapped herself to some unknown location. As if we didn't have enough to deal with.

The moments ticked by before she finally stepped out from the side of the cabin.

My jaw set to stone as I marched over to her. After grabbing her arm in my tight grip, I hurried her back to the front yard before letting her go.

"What the hell were you doing?" I asked, sounding as angry as I felt. That anger was bubbling at the surface. I blamed these days of being at high alert all the fucking time.

"I wanted to get some flowers I saw on the far side of the cabin." She held a bunch of wildflowers in her grip.

"What the hell were you thinking?" I snapped. "You can't just disappear. You can't go off on your own. Are you trying to get yourself killed or taken?"

Her green eyes widened. "I wasn't trying to do either of those things. I wanted some flowers. They're inside the wards. I figured I could run back inside if I saw anything weird. Or if anyone showed up."

"You thought... You can't be serious right now, Hazel." I stooped down to her level so that we were eye to eye. "What if you got scared and transported yourself to Siberia? How would I find you?"

Her mouth opened then closed again like she couldn't come up with an answer to that.

"Exactly. You need someone with you at all times."

She shook her head. "I'm not going to be babysat like that. What's next? Someone going to follow me into the bathroom?"

"If necessary."

She winced, like she hadn't known I'd thought of that already.

"Look, Miller, I didn't think it'd be a big deal. Two minutes on the other side of the cabin that's still within the wards. Nothing happened."

"But it could have," I snapped, then immediately wished I hadn't.

"Well, you're kind of being a dick right now, so I'm going to go back inside. Maybe it's all this together time or the pressure of what's going on, so I won't hold it against you." Her chin dropped to her chest. "But maybe you need a little more fresh air."

Hazel pushed the bunch of flowers into my chest and let go. I wasn't quick enough to catch them and they all fluttered to the ground. She kept walking toward the cabin and didn't glance back once.

The last thing I wanted was to hurt my girl's feelings, but she had to understand that absolute fear that ran through me every time she wasn't close by.

A therapist could retire on what we were going through right now.

I did stay outside. Long enough that eventually, everyone else came out.

Luken slid in beside me, but the others stayed back closer to the cabin. "We figured we should get as much training in as possible." He glanced at me and then back to the trees. "The fight's coming. We all know it. The women should be able to defend themselves."

"Yeah. You're right." I swallowed hard. "We can't rely on the four of us to protect them. Anything could happen."

"Exactly." He didn't speak for a moment, but him watching me was palpable, like I could feel every glance on my skin. "Everything OK?"

"Why wouldn't it be?"

"Hazel came into the cabin looking a little flushed with anger."

"How do you know it's anger?"

"I know." He cleared his throat. "What happened?"

"Nothing." The word came out of my mouth almost immediately before I turned to him. "You and Caleb should work with her today. Oliver and I will take on Nellie and Gia." Then I walked away.

I wanted nothing more than to help Hazel and be the one to teach her what she needed to know. But we'd established long ago that I wasn't the best option for that. When we'd first started training her on the craft, Oliver and Luken had had to give me a lecture about how I'd been too careful with her. They'd been right then and they'd be right now.

She needed someone who would push her for her own good.

And Caleb had given her some of his dark magic. Since he was the only who knew how that would work for her, he had to be involved.

It didn't matter how much I fucking hated it.

Once Luken and I had joined the others, I said, "Nellie, Gia, come on. Oliver and I are going to work with you today." Oliver raised an eyebrow in surprise while Hazel scowled.

"What about me?" she asked.

When my eyes settled on hers, I kept my emotions in check. This woman could feel others' feelings and hadn't learned how to block it yet, which meant it was up to me to make sure she couldn't read me so well.

"You're going to work with Caleb and Luken." Then I walked away, assuming that Nellie and Gia would follow.

It was hard being on the opposite side of the yard from her while someone else did what I was supposed to. Even worse was seeing Caleb or Luken touch her once in a while and it didn't matter that they were innocent necessary touches.

I had no idea what the fuck was wrong with me right now.

"OK." I clapped my hands together, like I was excited to get this started. "Let's get you two fully witched up."

"Is there any way to break our bindings?" Gia asked. "I've heard about a blood moon sacrifice or something."

Oliver snorted. "We don't have a blood moon or a sacrifice."

"That wouldn't work anyway," I told her. "I don't think, at least, and we shouldn't waste our time trying things we don't know will work. For you two, we're going to focus on spells. How to create and execute them on the fly because even bound, you can do that. We've also got a bunch of potions." I glanced at Oliver, who nodded. "We need to make sure you're familiar with what each one does. You can use those. We'll make you up some battle packs or something so you'll be able to protect yourselves."

"And help," Nellie added. When I didn't answer, she said, "We want to help. Nobody has come looking for us and we love Hazel. We want to help keep her safe too."

Nodding, I answered, "Well, this will do that, too. Let's get started."

The first thing we taught the two of them was the mechanics of a spell. Exactly what elements were needed to make it work. Then we had them try a few easy ones that we'd created for them. Make the grass grow. Wilt the flower. Easy shit like that.

Once they'd mastered casting the spells, it was time for them to start making some themselves. Again, easy ones. Had to take baby steps when it came to magic.

"What were you trying to do?" I asked, giving it my best to keep all the humor out of my voice.

Gia let her arms fall limply to her sides. "I was trying to break that bottle." She pointed to the glass bottle I'd set on the ground about three feet from us.

Instead of breaking, it fell over. Which was at least something.

Now that she knew what she wanted to do, I could work with her on perfecting it. Which we did.

We were at it for hours with only a brief break for lunch, during which Hazel stood on the other side of the table from me, quickly eating a sandwich and not saying a single word. To anyone.

I needed to apologize.

When we went back out for round two, I wrapped my hand around her bicep and pulled her to the side. She looked up at me with all the expecta-tions in her eyes.

"I'm sorry," I told her. "I was being a dick. You were right. With everything going on, I'm like a hypervigilant attack dog. I'm sorry. I'll keep it under check."

She swallowed and nodded. "I appreciate your apology and I understand. I'm sorry that I'm so much trouble and have made you a hypervigilant attack dog."

I snorted. "You didn't do this. *They* did this. With each passing day, I know a fight is growing closer. They've actually been too quiet, which means they're planning something and I hate that I don't know what. I can't stand the fact that you could get hurt."

"I don't really think I'm worth all of this trouble," she said, like she was confessing her darkest thoughts.

"You are. To me, you are. Because losing you would break me." I pulled her into my arms. "There's nothing I wouldn't do to protect you. You know, I've heard that the difference between the hero and the villain is that the hero would sacrifice the person they love to save the world and the villain would burn the world to save their love. If that's true, then I'm the villain," I told her and it was true. There was no one I wouldn't sacrifice for her, especially myself.

"Miller..." She pushed up to her toes so her lips could reach mine. It was the exact reassurance that I needed to know that we were OK. I'd been a dick earlier and she had forgiven me.

She wrapped a hand around the back of my head to pull me down as she lowered herself, but that wasn't enough. I slid an arm around her back and lifted so her feet weren't touching the ground at all. The way she felt against me, the way her mouth glided against mine had me wanting to take her back into the cabin and strip her naked.

And then someone cleared his throat far too close to us.

"So are we done training, then?" Oliver asked and by the sound of his voice, he was holding back the humor he found in this situation.

I let the kiss go, pulling Hazel back in for another moment when she tried to end it, before setting her back on her feet. Fuck him for interrupting that, but he was right. We needed to make sure the ladies had at least the bare minimum level of defense.

"Let's go," I told the two of them as I took Hazel's hand in mine.

"You should probably know that Luken and Caleb want me to try teleporting on purpose this afternoon."

"What?"

"I'm going to be holding on to Luken, so if I go, he'll go too," she said quickly. "They say if I can do it on purpose, then I can probably stop myself from doing it on accident."

That much was true, but fuck, did I hate the whole thing.

I didn't say anything about that plan because I fucking hated it, but it was something that had to be done. I'd just have to hate it from my side of the yard.

And I did.

While Oliver and I worked with Nellie and Gia, I kept glancing over at my girl. When the bright, white appeared, followed by her and Luken disappearing, I almost came unglued. Luckily, they were back moments later.

Hazel threw herself into Luken's arms with excitement and they all looked pretty proud of themselves. It'd take a while before she perfected it, but damn. She was a fast learner.

As the three of them continued working, we took Nellie and Gia into the house to work on potions.

We'd have to do this with Hazel as well, but for now, it was just the four of us. We were just lucky that Mom brought more potion supplies when she'd brought food. It wasn't everything but we'd make due.

At least the potions came with some laughter and it finally hit me why the coven often wanted Oliver, Luken, and me to help with training witches. We were natural teachers and were having a little bit of fun with it.

Until the world threatened to turn on its side.

Thunder cracked around us so loudly that it vibrated the windows of the cabin. Nellie and Gia shrieked at the sound and it startled the shit out of me too.

"What the hell was that?" Oliver asked. "It sounded like thunder, but..."

"That wasn't thunder." We both knew it wasn't.

That was the crack of powerful magic. When the next thunder-like clap hit all I could think of was Hazel. The two of us ran outside, dropping the potions we had in our hands, only to find the Dark Fae whom Hazel was supposed to marry standing just outside of our wards with her parents by his side.

14

HAZEL

"You're getting good at this," Luken told me as I blocked yet another of his emotions. I'd been able to zap him and me away and then back, but only once. He assured me that I'd get it, but it cost me a lot of energy to do and would take some time to perfect.

"One more?" Caleb asked, which had me nodding.

The better I got at this, the less everyone else would affect me.

Caleb narrowed his eyes on me and I threw up the shields that Luken had taught me to build. Soon, the shield would be up all the time and I'd have to remove it to know what someone was feeling. I liked the idea of that. Though the emotions thing had already started to fade and I wasn't sure if it was because the zapping thing required more energy, as they'd told me. Or if it was a fleeting power.

Eden hadn't thought so.

"I'm not picking up anything," I told him as he stared at me.

The corner of his mouth turned up, which then turned into a full smile. "Good. Miller would've kicked my ass for that one."

The guys chuckled as I shook my head. Now I was really glad I hadn't been able to feel what he'd been thinking.

"Tired?" Luken asked.

"Yeah. I wouldn't have thought being a witch would be so tiring."

Luken snorted. "It's why the guys and I are eating all the time."

Which was weird because I'd seen them eat while we'd been here, but barely. Caleb handed me a bottle of water, which I took happily. It was a warm day and the sun was out in full force. Even working underneath this large tree in the shade only helped with a couple of degrees.

When the loud crack of thunder threatened to put me on my ass, I welcomed the idea of rain. Maybe that would be enough to cool us off for a bit.

However, it only took one look at the guys to know that this wasn't regular thunder.

They both stiffened and spun around, their eyes moving left and right, like they were searching for something. Caleb tapped Luken then pointed to the trees.

A second thunderous crack ripped through the thick air.

That was when I saw him.

Or them.

A tall man with very dark hair that brushed his shoulders emerged from the treeline. He was wearing black jeans and a black T-shirt. All very emo. The darkness of his clothing make his skin seem pale with hardly a hint at color. He looked like he was in his thirties, and he was leading my parents as if they were on a leash.

The door to the cabin burst open with Miller and Oliver running toward us. Miller grabbed my wrists roughly then flung me behind him. As much as I wanted to burrow into his back and ignore everything that was happening, I couldn't. I wouldn't.

This was all because of me. I had to know what was happening.

The guys walked closer to the man and my parents, though I didn't want them to. But there was also no way we'd all hear each other from this far away. Still, they stopped pretty far from them. Before anyone said a word, Nellie and Gia were on either side of me.

"You're not going to touch her," Miller said and it was the first solid reason I had to understand that this man was the Fae whom I was supposed to marry. My stomach tightened as I curled my fingers into the back of his shirt. "You might as well leave."

A sly smile slid over the Fae's face. "I haven't come the kidnap her," he said, his voice sounding almost musical. Given that I'd had no interaction with a Fae in my life, the sound surprised me. He looked at me as if what he said wasn't true. As if he wanted to grab a hold of me and eat me up.

A shiver skittered up my spine and I thought I'd hid it until the Fae chuckled.

"Then why are you here?" Luken asked.

"To see if my betrothed would like to accept a deal."

He meant me and I hated that he did.

"She doesn't want any deal from you," Miller answered for me.

The Fae *tsked*. "I need to hear it from her." His dark, dead eyes settled on me again. "She should at least hear me out."

I took a big step forward, though I still felt Miller at my back ready to put me behind him if necessary. I loved that he was so protective and the idea that he'd sacrifice himself to keep me safe, but I really didn't want him to. Even if it came to that. I didn't want him sacrificing himself for me.

The Fae stepped over the line of protection, leaving my parents where they were. However, he snapped his fingers and they fell to their knees. That was when I knew they weren't there because they wanted to be. They didn't have a choice.

"Now, betrothed..." He stopped right before me. The way he referred to me had the acid in my stomach climbing my throat. It was like he didn't know my name, even though he had plans for me. "This is my offer and I don't negotiate. Your friends here will tell you that. It's yes. Or it's no."

"No," automatically came out of my mouth.

He let out a humorless chuckle while shaking his head. "Again, you have to hear the offer first."

"How did you cross the wards?"

"Silly witch." His index finger trailed down my

cheek, causing Miller's hand around my wrist to tighten. Things were about to get very ugly, but I figured there had to be a reason the guys hadn't attacked the Fae in the first place.

Deep down, I knew that going up against the Fae likely meant that we wouldn't all make it out of this.

"Wards don't work on me. Something your friends here should've explained. Now, the ruins with angel blood that your father tore down, that would've made me work for it. This... is nothing."

"What do you want?" I wanted this over as soon as possible.

"Well, I would've thought that was obvious," he told me. "I made a deal for a dark witch virgin and that's the payment I would have liked."

"I'm not a dark witch or a virgin."

His eyes darkened more. "This, I know." When he looked at Miller as if he were the one who'd kept him from receiving his virgin, all I wanted was the creature's eyes back on me. "A dark witch of angel descent would be good enough. The virgin part would've brought a stronger connection when I relieved you of that status, but we work with what we have, right?"

"I'm not a dark witch."

"Pity. I know that, though. So." He clapped his hands together and took a step back from me. "This is the new deal. You voluntarily come with me under the knowledge that you will become a dark witch and be my power source or... I kill you parents while you watch. A debt does need to be paid."

My heart raced.

There was no love lost between my parents and me, but I didn't want to be the cause of anyone's death. Even if they would've had no problem being the cause of mine.

"Hazel," Miller said at my hesitation.

But still, I didn't answer right away. I wanted this to be right. It wasn't until I found the words that portrayed exactly how I felt that I spoke. "The only family that I care about is the one behind me. I'm not going anywhere with you."

"Hazel," my father called out.

The Fae snapped his fingers and my father's angry voice was gone.

This man scared me, but I wouldn't let him know it.

His black eyes narrowed. "Are you sure about that? I will kill them."

"I know you will." I took a deep breath to calm my nerves. "I know you will and I don't want that.

But they didn't care enough about me not to sell me off, so their decisions bring their consequences. I'm not going with you."

"Pity." His eyes slid over me like a touch that I could feel, making me want to immediately take a shower. "It would've been a lot more fun with you."

Miller's muscles tensed and while I had my shields up to protect myself against what everyone was feeling, his feelings still creeped through.

The Fae shook his head and backed away.

"Say the word," Luken whispered so that only we could hear them.

"No." I held my hand up without turning around. "I don't think he's going to try to take me right now."

The Fae kept walking backward before spinning around and turning his back to us as if he didn't have a care in the world. He wasn't worried about what we might've done to him.

He stopped next to my parents and shook his head. His mouth was moving, but I couldn't hear what he was saying right before he lifted his hands and my parents began to scream.

Somehow, my father had his voice back.

Nellie and Gia startled and when I took a step forward, a large, strong hand stopped me.

"You can't go to them," Miller whispered against my ear. "Turn away. Don't watch, but you can't go."

Their screaming was endless, but I didn't turn away. I couldn't. Before I knew what was happening, a tear fell down my cheek.

Was it for my parents or was it because I'd never seen someone killed like that? I didn't know, but I never wanted to see it again.

I was about to turn away when my mother's gaze caught mine. Even though she was clearly in pain, the corners of her lips turned up. Just for a moment, I let my shield down to see if I could feel what she was.

She agreed with what I was doing. She sent out love but it was too late.

If only she had loved me more sooner.

My parents' bodies slumped to the ground and I staggered back into Miller. He righted me, making sure I was steady on my feet before the Fae got back to us.

"Just know, betrothed, there are consequences to every decision. I had to take your parents' powers as payment. Did I have to kill them?" He tapped a finger against his chin. "Maybe not. But they crossed me and I do not like to be crossed. Next time, I might not be so forgiving." He took a step away from me. "You'll clean up my mess, won't you?"

And then he was gone. My knees gave out, but Miller wouldn't let me fall.

"Come here." He pulled me into him and turned me away so I wasn't staring at the bodies of my parents. I was pressed against his chest as the rest of the group formed a circle around us.

"I'm OK," I told them as I put a little bit of room between Miller and me. Not much at all, but enough that I could speak. "They made their own beds and my father didn't love me. My mother went along with him. This is on them. I'm not sad. I'm not happy, but I'm not sad."

"You staggered," Miller pointed out. "What happened?"

"I don't know." Something hit me. Or that was what it had felt like. "It was like something pressed me back. Something against my chest. As if it had been pushing and I'd been resisting. Then it won. I don't know what that was."

"The unbinding," Gia offered. "With her father..." She glanced at where my parents lay. "All of her would be unbound now. It was her full powers hitting."

"She's right," Oliver agreed. "That has to be it."

"Great." I threw my hands in the air. "Does that mean I have more powers waiting to hit me?"

Luken spoke first. "Not necessarily. It could just mean the full power of your abilities will hit. We'll have to wait and see."

"I don't get it," Caleb told us. "That was... anticlimactic. This was what we were running from and fighting? Hazel could've just said *no* the whole time? I'm not buying it."

"Neither am I," Miller agreed.

"So he's coming back?" Nellie asked.

"I don't think so," I told them. "He felt... very done with me when I said I wasn't coming."

"But he said that choice had consequences. That next time he wasn't going to play as nicely."

That was true. But again, I'd let the Fae's feelings in, so I'd know when he was planning to attack and I'd felt... nothing. He didn't want me anymore.

"Maybe the power from my parents was enough?" It was a stupid dream for that to be true, but all I had was hope right now.

"Or he's got a backup plane," Oliver offered and the thought turned my stomach.

Another witch or angel could be in danger.

"I guess that's a problem for another day," Luken told us. "A problem that might not even be Hazel's.

Maybe the consequence he was talking about is that he has a different plan now. One that none of us are going to like."

Now that was easy to buy.

"For now," Caleb said, cutting in, "we have a mess to clean up." He nodded toward my parents and that wasn't something I looked forward to at all.

They had once been my only connection in this world and now they were gone. I couldn't be sorry about that, but I could mourn what I didn't have and now, never would.

"Hey." Miller pulled me away from the group. "You all right? I mean you're not, obviously. This was a lot."

I reached a hand up to cup his hard jaw. "I'm OK. As OK as I can be, but they never felt like family to me. You do." I took a deep breath. "I'm sure I'll have to process this all at some point, but right now, I don't feel much about it."

"OK." He pulled me into his arms and kissed the top of my head. "We have to clean this up. We can't leave them there."

"Right." I pulled away. "I really don't want that, but I also can't watch."

"Of course not. You should take Nellie and Gia inside. We'll handle this."

And that was exactly what I did.

The three of us were in the house, looking over the potions wondering if, since this had turned into a big nothing, what the next shit to hit the fan would be.

And who would be the one to catch it.

15

MILLER

THERE WERE two dead bodies that we needed to take care of. We couldn't leave them there, clearly, even if they hadn't been Hazel's parents.

But they were and we needed to figure out what to do with them.

I watched the women go back inside the cabin, hoping that Hazel would fight the urge to watch out the window. Right now, she insisted she was unaffected, but eventually, feelings were going to kick in. Which was why I wanted to get this done as soon as possible so that I could be there when it happened.

"What're we going to do with them?" Luken asked after the door to the cabin closed. "Bury them?"

Oliver groaned at the prospect of having to dig

graves. It was what we were all thinking, but we'd do it if we needed to.

"I don't know," I answered. "I'm not sure that's the best option. I mean, we'd have to dig pretty far and it would have to be inside the wards, which I don't love. In the woods would be rough and someone might come across their bodies one day."

"Burn them," Caleb offered, which brought all of our attention to him. We'd been in this situation before when we'd been on jobs for the coven, but then we'd had a cleanup crew who'd taken care of everything. Now we didn't. "Like Viking funeral pyres. It's the best option. No one's going to find the Rileys in a shallow grave later. We get rid of them now so Hazel's not staring at her parents' dead bodies."

"It is kind of perfect." Luken looked at me. It was my decision, but really, I didn't think it was.

"Let me talk to Hazel real quick. I don't think she's going to care, but I want to ask."

The three of them murmured their agreement as I headed into the cabin, where the women were. The three of them were on the couch with Hazel in the middle. It looked like Nellie and Gia were comforting her, though Hazel still looked like she had outside. Not upset and a tiny, little smile curved her lips.

"Can I talk to you for a minute?" I asked.

Hazel's gaze found me quickly and she nodded. But as she moved to get up, I dropped onto the coffee table and took her hands in mine.

"We've come up with a solution to..."

"My parents?"

"Yeah. But I wanted to run it by you first." I took a deep breath as I glanced at both Nellie and Gia. They'd made no motion to leave us alone and I hadn't asked them to. "We decided that burying them is a bad idea. Someone could... find them one day. Caleb suggested a funeral pyre. How do you feel about that?"

She blinked twice before cocking her head to the side. "Burn them?"

"Yeah. That's one way to describe it."

"That's fine with me, Miller. Whatever you have to do is fine with me."

I narrowed my eyes on her. "Are you sure?"

"Yeah. I'm pretty numb to it all right now, so whatever you need to do, do it. This will erase all traces of their magic too, right?" she asked. I furrowed my brows. "That's what Gia said. If they had any magical items on them, this would get rid of that, right?"

I wet my lips quickly while holding back how crazy I thought it was that Hazel didn't have any strong feelings about what was going on right now. It was weird.

Until I realized what was happening.

My jaw clenched with anger as I pushed up from my spot without answering Hazel and marched back out of the cabin. I wasn't even close to the guys before I called out. "What are you doing?"

Luken hopped between us with the stance of a man who thought he was about to stop a freight train with his bare hands. As if I wouldn't go through him if I needed to. Right now, I just wanted to get to the bottom of all this.

Caleb's eyebrows went up in surprise, as if he had no idea that I was talking to him. But I absolutely was.

"What are you doing to her?"

That was the moment he knew exactly what I meant. "Helping," he said, as if that were supposed to mean dick to me.

"*Helping*?" I yelled.

"What's going on?" Oliver also wedged himself in close to us, like he thought it might take the both of them to stop me from getting to Caleb now that they knew it was about Hazel.

I pushed forward, causing both of them to grab a shoulder and move me back.

"I'm helping," Caleb said slowly. "This is a lot to deal with for any of us. I didn't want her falling apart."

I clenched my teeth together. It was the only thing I could think to do so I didn't punch this guy in the face. "What. Are. You. Doing. To. Her?"

"Nothing," he insisted. When I growled he held up a hand. "Nothing bad. When the Fae killed her parents, I cast a little spell that will help keep her from freaking out."

"'Help keep her from freaking out'?" I yelled again, then I took a step away from Oliver and Luken. "It's not helping her from freaking out. She's fucking *numb*, as if her parents dying doesn't affect her. Now, I understand they had a shitty relation-ship, but I don't think she's ever seen two people killed in front of her before. It *should* affect her."

"I was trying to help."

"Don't put spells on my girlfriend." Now I got around both Luken and Oliver so that I could stand almost toe to toe with the bastard. Maybe they understood now that whatever I did to Caleb, he deserved it. "Remove it. You don't do shit like that to her, period, and certainly not without talking to her and me first."

Though I would've told him to fuck off if he had talked to me about it.

"Right now?" He didn't move away from me at all. He wasn't scared of me and probably didn't think that I'd rip his head off and normally I wouldn't. But this was about Hazel. "You want me to remove the spell right now when we're about to burn her parents' bodies?"

Well, fuck. When he put it like that... Sure, I was pissed he'd done this in the first place. That didn't mean I wanted Hazel to be in the house with feelings flooding her when I couldn't be there for her.

"No." That was the decision I'd come to. "When we're done. But, Caleb..." I gave him a menacing glare. "Don't fucking do this again."

Brother or not, cousin or not, I'd kill him for fucking with her again.

With a simple nod of his head, we now had a job to do.

The four of us spread out to find as much wood as we possibly could. It took several trips from the trees before we had even close to the amount we needed to create the size of the fire that would be required. Luken had chosen the far corner of my parents' property that was still within the wards. This way, other people wouldn't necessarily notice anything going on.

Then we built the pyre.

It dawned on me that not everyone would know how to do this, but between the four of us, we seemed to work smoothly. First we built the base up then created almost a box out of tree limbs with the intention of putting the bodies inside and lighting it on fire.

Once we were satisfied, Caleb took the legs and Luken the arms of Hazel's dad while I took the legs and Oliver the arms of her mom.

This fucking sucked. Glad I wasn't on the regular cleanup crew.

We got them over and with quite a bit of effort dumped them inside.

Maybe this wasn't exactly how the Vikings would've done it, but we'd given it our best.

"Ready to light it?" Oliver asked, but I shook my head.

"I'm going to make sure Hazel doesn't want to be here." Then I turned and jogged back to the house.

The women were still on the couch like they hadn't moved and this was when I realized that

Caleb hadn't only spelled Hazel. Nellie and Gia hadn't had much of a reaction, either. *Damn it.*

"Hazel," I said gently. "It's time. Do you want to be out there?"

At first, she shook her head, but then she pushed to her feet. "You know what? I think I will be out there. It's only right."

Right now, she wasn't making a lot of sense to me. I figured that it was because her feelings weren't making a lot of sense to her, given that they were funneled through Caleb's spell.

I took her hand in mine, but she immediately pulled it back, so I set mine on her lower back to lead her out to the pyre with Nellie and Gia behind us.

"Ready?" Oliver asked. I gave him the go-ahead.

He snapped his fingers, creating a spark that he threw at the pyre. Then he walked around and repeated the process around the structure.

"You can create fire with the snap of your fingers?" Hazel asked him in awe, as if that were what she should've been focused on right now.

"It's a spell," he told her. One that was actually pretty easy to learn if she really wanted to.

Hazel looked down at her own hand and

snapped her fingers. Then she did it again, like she didn't understand why fire wasn't appearing.

This spell of Caleb's was fucking with her and it needed to end right now.

"Hazel." Those big, green eyes slowly looked up at me. "I have to tell you something. Caleb put a spell on you so you wouldn't have big feelings about what happened to your parents."

She cocked her head to the side and furrowed her brows. "Why would he do that? I didn't like my parents."

"I know." I ran a hand down her arm. "That doesn't mean you wouldn't feel a thing about the fact that you just watched them be killed by a dark Fae." I glanced at Nellie and then Gia. "I think he spelled the two of you as well."

"Well, I feel violated." Gia giggled. Obviously, I was right. This wasn't normal for any of them.

"I'm going to have him remove the spell," I told them all, but I focused on Hazel.

She glanced around nervously. "Does it have to be out here? In front of everyone? What if I lose it? That would be embarrassing, given that my parents didn't even like me."

I moved in close so that I could take her in my arms. "It wouldn't be embarrassing, but no. It doesn't have to be out here. We'll go inside, then he can come back out to take it off the other two."

Asking Caleb wasn't necessary. He'd do it if he knew what was good for him.

Which he did because he followed Hazel and me into the house. Once the door was closed behind us, his eyes settled on Hazel, then he whipped his hand around quickly and as her face fell, I knew the spell was gone.

Caleb got out of there pretty quickly, leaving us alone.

"Are you all right?" I asked.

"I think so," she whispered. "I thought I was just processing everything really well, but…"

"Not the case?" I asked. She shook her head quickly. "I promise, I didn't know he was going to do that. Hell, I didn't know he had until a little while ago."

"Now I'm not sure what to feel." She wrapped her arms around herself, which made me wrap mine around her too.

"You feel whatever you need to. It's OK if you're not super upset about what happened to them. It's also OK if you are. You feel whatever you need to."

"They didn't love me, Miller. Well, maybe my

mother did a little." Her voice was watery, as if she were about to cry but was fighting it.

"I love you enough for everyone."

I held her like that for a few minutes before Nellie and Gia came bursting through the door. They wedged themselves between us, creating a group hug that included the three of them.

"I can't believe that happened," Gia said, her voice wavering.

This was about seeing the Reillys killed. That would be enough to send anyone over the edge.

Their three voices filled the cabin as they relived it, going over what had happened and what they thought about it. It was their first time processing all of this, so I'd wait patiently.

But tears never came from Hazel. There was that moment when she'd sounded like she might cry, but that moment had passed and now, it was chatter. Like telling the story of a horrible accident you'd just happened to witness.

At least now they were feeling it and could deal with it.

And I'd be here if Hazel fell apart.

16

HAZEL

In some ways, I wished Caleb's spell could've stayed cast forever.

No. I understood why making me numb to the world around me was bad, especially since now that it was gone, I realized it had also hampered my feelings for Miller.

I loved Miller with everything that I was, but while that spell had been cast over me, he'd seemed fine, but the intense feelings had been gone.

It would've been bad to live the rest of my life like that.

But I couldn't be mad at Caleb for doing it. He'd just wanted to make things easier for me. Though I decided to tell him never to do it again with my permission. Gia might've been joking when she said she felt violated but that was kind of true.

However, having all these conflicting emotions coursing through me wasn't great, either.

Was I sad that my parents were dead?

Not really. They hadn't shown me love for most of my life. Now I understood that they'd likely been protecting themselves. I mean, why get attached when they were going to hand me over to a dark fae? What would have been the point?

If they had loved me, wanted me, they wouldn't have made the deal in the first place. Yes, I understood that they hadn't thought I'd exist when they'd made the deal, but fuck. I couldn't imagine looking down at a tiny baby face knowing that I was only going to raise her like a pig to be slaughtered.

I'd never know what they'd been thinking and maybe that was the worst part of it.

"You OK?" Miller asked as he quietly shut the door behind him.

I shrugged. "I think I'm as OK as I can be." But I didn't look over at him.

It wasn't that long ago that I'd thought Miller hated me, had always hated me. So, I guess, there was one thing that I'd gained from this whole experience.

Him. And there was no doubt in my mind that I had him, just as he had me.

I'd also gained his family, his friends, and some witchy powers that I didn't quite understand yet.

Miller came across the room and dropped to his knees in front of where I was sitting on the edge of the bed. "You know you don't have to be, right?"

"Be what?" I raised my eyes to meet his.

"All right. You don't have to be. If you need to fall apart, you can."

I gave him a sad smile. "I can't really do that, can I? It's not really the time, right? Anything could happen and while I'm pretty useless on a good day, falling apart would make it worse."

He pushed my hair away from my face then cupped my cheek. "I'd make sure no one got to you. You do what you need to do."

This wasn't a side of Miller I'd ever expected to see until recently. He'd been such an asshole to me in high school that I'd gone years trying to avoid him. Now, he was taking care of me in my darkest moments. I'd do the same for him.

"I feel bad." I finally confessed the thing I'd only thought up till this point.

He pulled away from me and sat back on his legs. "What do you have to feel bad about?"

"My parents died, Miller, and I don't feel strongly about that. I'm not crying. Aren't you supposed to cry when your parents die? *You* would, right?"

He nodded slowly. "I would, but my parents aren't like yours. Yours don't deserve your tears. If you wanted to give them, fine. But you aren't required to."

"Worst of all, outside of feeling... numb, I almost feel... relieved." My eyes burned with tears I wouldn't let fall. Those weren't for my parents. Those were because I felt guilty about that relief.

Who felt relieved when their parents died? Me, because with them burning outside, at least there was one less threat to the people I cared about.

"How fucked-up is that?" I asked him quietly.

"It's not." He brought both of his hands back up to cup my face. His fingers pushed into my hair. "It's not fucked-up. They were a threat to you and I'm relieved, too."

"But they weren't your parents."

"They don't deserve anything other than what they got. They're the ones who made the deal with the dark Fae. That shit never turns out OK. They were the greedy ones. Selfish, and it came back to bite them in the ass. That's on them. You didn't do anything."

"I know." I blew out a breath as he slid his hands over my shoulders and down my arms then rested them on my thighs. "I think Caleb's spell is still messing with me. Like I think I'm supposed to feel certain things and I'm not, but I was completely numb to everything—even you—a couple of minutes ago."

Miller pushed to his feet and paced in front of me as he rubbed his index finger over his bottom lip. When he stopped, he turned to me. "What do you mean 'even to me'?"

I swallowed hard. He wasn't going to love this.

"When I was under the spell, I still knew I loved you, but I didn't *feel* it. I didn't feel much of anything, honestly."

Miller's jaw tensed. "I'm sorry I didn't realize he'd done it earlier."

"Not your fault." I pushed to my feet and took the three steps needed so that I'd be in his space. "Now it's like I'm waiting to feel things again. I mean, I'm feeling things. I *feel* that I love you. I *feel* guilty. But it's like it's still a little far away. I'm sure that will wear off, right?"

"It better or Caleb's going to have some more explaining to do."

I allowed a quiet laugh to leave my chest. Those

two would probably be working on their relation-
ship for a while. Spelling me without telling anyone
was something that would make a person lose
Miller's trust. And I had a feeling once you lost that,
it was very hard to get back.

"I have an idea," I told him, which caused him to
raise an eyebrow. When I pushed my hands under
his T-shirt and slid my fingers over his warm stomach, his breath hissed between his teeth. "I *think* you
could help with that?"

"With what?"

"Making me feel." As if I hadn't just said that
word a hundred times in the last few minutes. It was
starting to lose all meaning. "I've been numb and
think I need something to break through the barrier.
Bring all of my emotions to the surface. I think
you're the one to do that."

Miller swallowed hard and brought his hands to
rest on each side of my neck and stroked his thumbs
across my cheeks. "I'm definitely the one to do that.
But are you sure, Hazel?"

"I want nothing more than to be surrounded by
you." I pushed my hands farther up his chest. "Want
nothing more than to block out all the shit on the
other side of that door so that it's only you and me,
at least for a little while."

I'd barely gotten the words out when his mouth crashed over mine.

Miller was gentle in his kisses, but something about it made me realize that he was holding back and that was the last thing I wanted him to do. I wanted everything without any hesitation from him. Even though he was likely being gentle out of concern for me. Like I wouldn't be able to handle it. Yet gentle wasn't what I needed.

I pushed back against his gentle kisses with more forceful ones of my own. He responded in kind. His lips were rough against mine as his hands slid around to cup my ass. I pressed into him, as if I thought I could actually climb inside him. Not even daylight could get between us.

He moved us back toward the bed, but before I hit it, he yanked my shirt over my head and quickly undid my bra. Before he could kiss me again, I pushed at his shirt. He was so much taller than me that I couldn't get it off myself. He had to help. Our chests were skin to skin when we fell back onto the bed.

Which wasn't nearly naked enough.

With Miller dropping wet kisses down my body until he got to my breasts and took a nipple into his mouth, I was able to do exactly what I'd wanted.

Block out the world that existed outside of this bedroom.

I groaned as my eyes fluttered shut when he scraped his teeth over my sensitive skin then let the nipple audibly pop from his mouth. Then he kissed down my stomach until he got to the button on my jeans. That was when he moved off me.

Missing his weight against me was a given, but if this was to go where I wanted it to, it was a small price to pay.

He popped the button on my jeans and pulled them down my legs, slipping my shoes off as he went. Then he gave my panties a yank and I was laid out in front of him completely naked.

Yet I wasn't self-conscious at all.

There was some movement that I assumed was him taking off his own pants, though I didn't look. My eyes were still closed in anticipation of what he was going to do next.

The bed dipped under his weight before he pushed my legs apart. Then his mouth was on me. Gentle at first again, as if he were testing the waters to make sure I wasn't going to freak out, but this was one thing I'd never freak out over.

Being with Miller was safe.

His big hands held my thighs apart so that every

time I tightened, I didn't squeeze his head. He lapped at me with purpose. Pushing a finger inside me almost caused my orgasm to rip through me, but I wasn't there yet. As he licked and sucked and scraped his teeth against my most sensitive area, it was like the fog Caleb had created began to lift.

With each move, my feelings crashed over me. The fact that anything, even a spell, could make me not feel the love that I had for Miller was astounding and showed just how powerful the magic was. I could've gone my whole life just knowing that I loved him without this overwhelming need for him and that would've been a half-life.

The complete love we had for each other was a gift. Not something to be wasted or pushed aside, even if Caleb had thought it'd been for my own good.

My orgasm crashed over me like waves in the ocean hitting the sandy beach. Waves that I wished would never end. When the water calmed, Miller bit into my right thigh then soothed it with his tongue and while normally, I didn't really want to be bitten, this... this was different.

"You good?" he asked once he'd climbed back up. His hardness pressed against my clit. I nodded and knew what the little satisfied grin on my face looked like because I'd seen it in the mirror when he and I'd been together before. "Gonna need you to say it."

I forced my eyes to open. "I'm more than good, Miller."

He leaned down and kissed me before grabbing a condom from the dresser and rolling it on. His mouth was back on me when he pushed inside me in one stroke, causing my eyes to close again.

"Not this time." He didn't move. "Open your eyes, Hazel."

I groaned but did as he'd commanded. Then he thrust into me again. When my eyes rolled back into my head, he stopped again. "Eyes open."

I shook my head but did it again. This time, though it took all of my focus, I kept my eyes on him while he fucked me. I pressed my hands against the wall behind me and arched my back.

With Miller, I didn't have to do much to make it feel good for either of us. He'd told me once that he was just grateful to be invited to the party, but I wanted to play my part. I wanted to be for him what he was for me.

After taking my hands away from the wall, I grabbed on to his broad shoulders and dug my nails into him. I wouldn't leave scars, but this man knew how to make me feel... well, everything.

Given what had happened today, we weren't going to be changing positions or anything like that. Face to face was the most intimate and personal and that was what we both needed. He dropped his forehead to mine as he pushed toward his own release.

"I love you, Miller," I whispered, causing his mouth to cover mine again only moments before he found the release he'd been chasing.

Both of us were breathing quickly when he rolled off me. He gave me two more quick kisses before he headed to the bathroom to take care of things. When he returned, I did the same thing and then put some pajamas on before climbing back into bed with him.

I didn't care what time of day it was. I was exhausted and would be going to sleep.

"You didn't have to get dressed," he told me when I snuggled against his bare chest.

"Sure, I did. I'm about to pass out and would hate for someone to accidentally come in here while I'm still naked."

He snorted. "No one's coming in here when they know exactly what we were doing."

I pushed up in surprise. "What do you mean? Yeah, they might assume, but they don't *know*."

Miller gave me a big grin. "You were kind of loud. I'm pretty sure they know."

My face burned with embarrassment. "I was loud. I didn't say anything."

"Not words, I guess."

I slapped a hand over my face and slid back down so I wouldn't have to look at him. "I swear I didn't make a weird noise."

Once he'd stopped laughing, he said, "It's fine, Hazel. Normally, no, you aren't loud, but you were today and that's OK."

I groaned. "No. It's not. Now everyone knows that I watched my parents burn then immediately had sex with my boyfriend. That's weird."

He pulled the hand away from my face and lifted my chin so I'd have to look at him. "It's not weird," he assured me, but I scoffed. Of course it was. "But I don't give a shit what they know. What I care about is whether or not that fogginess is gone."

Oh. Right. The reason I'd wanted him right then. Well, not the entire reason, but part of the reason. "Completely gone. I'm once again consumed with love and desire for you. I feel it. I don't just know it."

"Perfect." He dropped a kiss to the tip of my nose then released me so that I could get comfortable again. "Exactly what I wanted."

The two of us were quiet for a while—how long, I didn't know—before I said, "No one's ever really wanted me."

His body stiffened. "I think I just proved you wrong on that."

"No one until you." I turned even more and propped my chin on his chest. "My family... what limited family I did have never wanted me. I didn't think you wanted me until recently. Most of the people at school didn't want me around."

"Hazel." He stopped me from continuing to highlight my pathetic life. "I wanted you then. I couldn't have you, though. And trust me, others wanted you."

"For more than just sex?" Because that was too easy.

"Yes. People in school... they wanted to be friends with you and you had friends. But a lot of us were intimidated by you or they were intimidated by me and I'm sorry for that." He paused to swallow hard. "You're clear that I want you for more than just sex, right?"

"Yes," I said immediately. Maybe too immediately.

"I hope that's true," he told me. "My parents want you. You're part of the family now, just like Luken and Oliver... and I guess Caleb since he's apparently blood-related." That was going to take some getting used to. "And I hope that soon you'll be ready to be officially part of my family since you already are."

I furrowed my brows then propped myself up on my elbow next to him. "What do you mean, 'officially'?"

He smiled and ran his hand down the side of my face. "I'm hoping that one day soon, you'll be ready to marry me."

Still confused, I asked, "Are you asking me to marry you?"

"No," he said, as if none of this was totally embarrassing. "I'm not asking you to marry me because that would be a shit thing to do right now, given everything that's going and everything that's already happened. This is me telling you that I want to marry you and one day when we're past all of this shit and you're ready, I'm going to ask."

"So you're letting me know that you're going to ask?" I cocked my head to this side. "Like it's a promise to ask one day?"

He chuckled, the action vibrating his chest and me, creating a warmth that I'd never known before. "I guess you can say that."

I leaned in and kissed him softly, but his hand on the back of my head held me there. When I pulled back, I whispered, "I guess this is my promise to say *yes*, then."

Miller pulled me back against him and at the very least I was sure I'd always have him. Him and his family and his friends.

I wouldn't be alone again.

17

───────

MILLER

Hazel had promised to say *yes*.

That was more than I ever could've hoped for. I'd promised to ask her to marry me when she was ready and we weren't in the middle of a bullshit nightmare and she'd promised to say *yes*.

I lay there awake until I knew she was asleep then headed to the kitchen to grab a drink of water. There was no chance I was going to leave while her eyes were still open.

After yanking on the jeans that I'd just taken off, I left the room as quietly as possible. Zipped but not buttoned, the jeans hung low on my hips and I didn't bother with a shirt because I was taking off what little clothing I had on as soon as I got back.

When I got over to the sink and turned it on so it

would get cold, Luken's voice came from the couch. "Things better now?"

"Yup." I grabbed a glass and filled it.

"Sounded like it."

I snorted. I'd told Hazel she'd been a little loud. Normally, she wasn't, but I guess getting your feelings back was powerful.

"I'm not sorry about that." I turned to rest my ass back against the edge of the counter and drained half the glass.

Luken chuckled as he got up and came closer, though the table was still between us. "Gia thought you were hurting the poor girl."

A bunch of the water I was trying to drink sprayed up into my face and dropped down my chest. "Fuck." I set down the glass and grabbed the nearest towel to dry myself off with. "I definitely wasn't hurting her."

"That's what I told Gia." He laughed quietly again. "I'm not sure she's experienced that to know the difference, so I told her those were good sounds. She turned bright red and shuffled off to their bedroom. Haven't seen her since."

"Hazel was numb," I explained. "Caleb removed that fucking spell, but she still felt like she was underwater. Knowing her feelings, feeling them slightly, but not experiencing them. So she could've tried to fully deal with her parents' deaths right then or—"

"Or you could fuck feelings into her?" He held back a grin as I shook my head.

"That's not how I would've put it, but sure."

"We don't care, Miller. She's good now, though, right? Whatever Caleb did is gone?"

"Seems like it."

"Then her parents' deaths are going to hit her."

He was right. "I know." There wasn't a damn thing I could do to stop it, either. "Nothing I can do about that other than be there for her, but right now, she's OK. She's so fucking sweet that she feels bad she's not sadder about it, too. Like, what the fuck? Her parents fucked her over in the worst way. They don't deserve her tears."

He nodded in agreement and folded his arms over his chest. "They don't. Doesn't mean they won't get them. Hell, people grieve what they're missing out on. Shit they didn't have the chance to experience. People who fucking abandoned them. Grief doesn't make sense."

Right there, I knew he was talking about himself and the father he'd never known. That used to bother him. More before he'd ever come to Echo

Valley, but still. He'd grieved a father he'd never even met.

"I know. And I'll be there when she needs me. She'll work through it."

Luken stepped around the table and came closer so that he could put a hand on my shoulder and squeeze. "I know you will be. She's lucky to have you."

I shook my head. "I'm lucky to have her."

"Damn right you are, but, Miller... Maybe next time don't make her friends worry about her safety."

The two of us laughed at the same time. Louder than we should have, given that there were people asleep in this cabin. But it felt like before all this shit had happened. Before I'd had Hazel. Before that piece of shit Michael had sent me to her, though I still didn't understand why he had.

"You're an asshole," I told him.

He held up his hands in self-defense. "I'm just saying what we're all thinking. Save that shit until you're back in your own apartment."

After giving him a shove, I headed back to the bedroom, where I shucked off all my clothes and climbed back into bed with the woman I loved.

The assurance that Hazel and I were on the same page when it came to our relationship was probably the reason I slept so well. It was like I'd closed my eyes two minutes ago and now it was morning, which I knew by the sunlight fighting its way around the shade on the window.

I rolled over to pull my girl closer, only to be left with a handful of sheet. She wasn't there and I tried not to let that freak me out.

We'd been through this before. She was either in the bathroom or the kitchen, I told myself. Her parents weren't a threat anymore. The Dark Fae had fucked off to whatever nasty hole he lived in, and the wards would alert me and the guys to any of the Dark Coven.

We were still fine.

Still, I couldn't just go back to sleep when I didn't know where she was, so I pushed up, yanked on my jeans from last night and headed for the door. As I made my way to the kitchen, I pulled my T-shirt down my chest with one hand and carried my shoes in the other.

"Morning," Caleb said, though he was quiet about it. With everyone else sleeping, there was no reason to be noisy.

"Morning."

He was already fully dressed in jeans and a T-shirt. Hell, he looked ready for the day. He'd even brushed his dark hair, whereas I didn't give a fuck if mine looked messy. It was a reminder of Hazel's fingers messing it up.

Caleb set a cup of coffee in front of me as I dropped into a chair to put my shoes on. "Thanks," I told him, then I took that first delicious drink. Damn, that was good coffee.

"So are we good?" he asked.

That was the question, wasn't it? Could I be good with a witch who'd cast a spell on my girl without either of us knowing? Even if it had been to help her, that was bullshit and could've had some terrible consequences.

"You ever going to cast a spell like that without telling us? Because that was some bullshit, but also, you could've ruined everything for her." My icy-blue eyes met his dark eyes and I hoped to hell that the fact that I still wanted to rip his head off for his actions came through loud and clear.

He furrowed his brows in confusion. "No. I won't. But what are you talking about, ruining everything? I was trying to help her. It was a lot to take all at once."

"I know it was." I took another slow drink. "I was prepared to help her through it, but you turned her into this pod person who not only wasn't experiencing any emotion around her parents' deaths, but she wasn't feeling anything. For anyone."

"What?" he asked, still clearly confused.

I sighed. This wasn't something I'd originally planned to share with him, but here we were. "She wasn't feeling anything. As she explained, she knew she loved me but didn't have a single significant feeling about it. Was that your intention?"

"No." He sat in a chair across from me. "I didn't intend for that to happen. Why would I?"

"Maybe you want her for yourself."

He chuckled. "I told you that wasn't the case. I told her that I offered to be with her before I knew she was betrothed to the Fae because I thought I could protect her. I wanted to protect her. I didn't want to f—I never wanted her like that." He took a drink. "Still don't. However, she's my friend, which I think bugs the shit out of you. You might want her like that. It doesn't mean every guy does."

He had me there. In my head, I couldn't imagine someone not wanting Hazel, but he was right. Oliver and Luken didn't want her like that.

"Look." He adjusted his weight like he was uncomfortable, but it wasn't the conversation doing it. That much, I was sure of. "I had good intentions with Hazel. Then and now. I wanted to get her out of there, but if I couldn't, I wanted to protect her. That's it. I know better than anyone what the Shadow Coven can do. As for the numbing spell, I've never had it affect someone like that. Maybe I got sloppy in my spell, but either way, it won't happen again."

"OK. I believe you." But did I trust him? It wasn't like I had much choice. Besides… "We're family, right? Which means she's your family now too because she is sure as fuck is *my* family."

"Exactly." He sat back, as if the conversation had lifted a weight that he'd been carrying around. "That's a weird thought, though. Family."

"Not used to having one, right?"

He nodded. "No. Mom… Well, you know about that. So all I've ever had is people willing to take care of me. Didn't make them family."

"Right. Well, Mom and Dad are the best you could hope for. Me… probably less so." Before he could ask the question I could see forming on his face, I answered it. "I'm not as good as they are. Like, they're genuinely good people who will do whatever they can to help someone else. I do that, but not like them. And I'm a lot more selfish than they are."

"How so?"

"Because I'd burn the world if it meant Hazel was safe. That's not exactly a *good person* thing."

"I don't know." He took a drink before continuing. "Seems like your dad's the same way, right? Didn't he do everything to protect your mom?"

They must've told him about that when they'd been here, but I hadn't realized he knew. Did that mean...?

"Did you know that Michael's the one who got my mom pregnant? I mean, did you know before you got here?"

"No." He swallowed hard. "I knew they did some shady shit, but I didn't always know what and that whole plan of breeding new members hasn't been something they've done in a long time. Or at least not on that scale because it took too long and didn't really work." His eyes met mine. "I mean, I guess except for me."

Shit. Right. He'd been born the same way I had

"Well, we're going to take care of him and all of the other Shadow Coven plants in our coven, right? Even if we can't take out the whole of your coven—"

"They're not my coven."

"You know what I mean. If we can't take them all out, we're at least going to get them out, of course." Then something else dawned on me. "I never asked. Is there anyone in your old coven you'd want to try to convert before..." I let that hang out there in the air because we both knew what the end plan was.

"No. Not really. I wasn't kidding when I said I didn't get close to pretty much anyone." He sighed. "I guess Juniper for the ladies' sake, but I don't think it would work. She's committed to staying to protect her brother."

While nodding, I took another quick drink of my coffee. "How about when it comes to it, we'll give her the option and promise to get her brother out? He's younger, so he wouldn't have committed yet. It'd be pretty easy."

"Sounds like a plan."

I was about to say something else when an uneasy warmth spread across my skin. Caleb's gaze jumped to mine as his jaw tensed and I knew he felt it too. We both understood what this meant.

I knew that feeling and it wasn't good.

That was the alert that something or someone had approached the wards and since we had spelled it to let us know when dark magic was near, I snapped to my full height.

I'd been out here a while and Hazel still hadn't come out. I hurried to the bedroom and pushed it open so hard that it hit the wall with a loud bang. Hazel still wasn't there.

"How long has Hazel been in the bathroom?" I asked.

Caleb furrowed his brows. "She's not in the bathroom. I was in there before you came out and your door was the only one that was open."

Fuck, fuck, fuck.

There was only one other place that Hazel could be.

Outside, where the danger was.

I was already on my way to the door when I told him, "Get Luken and Oliver. I think we're going to need all the help we can get."

I yanked open the door and stepped out into the early morning sunlight ready to start my day with a little murder.

18

HAZEL

THERE WAS something urging me to go outside.

Deep down, I knew I shouldn't go out there with everything going on. Or at least, I should wake Miller and get him to go with me. But he was sleeping so soundly, looking like a little boy with his relaxed face, and it wasn't relaxed at all when he was awake.

I hated that I was the cause of all these problems. Scratch that. I wasn't the case, but it had all been because of me. The Shadow Coven was the cause.

This pull to go outside was more of a feeling like I needed fresh air. We had charged wards up. One of the guys would have known if those had been broken, right?

My restlessness got the better of me, so I quietly got out of bed and pushed my feet into the Converse tennis shoes nearest my bed. My pajamas were a cotton tank top and shorts, which basically looked like something I'd wear outside anyway, so I didn't bother with getting dressed.

Outside, everything was peaceful. The sun was up, though not as high as it would get. The air was calm and tinged with the slightest hint of rain. Whether it was yet to rain or already had, I didn't know. The grass still had the dewiness that would have been there either way. It could've been rain that had made everything damp. I didn't know and my morning brain wasn't going to spend time processing it.

I wrapped my arms around myself at the cooler breeze of the morning, though there was no doubt it'd be heating up.

The one thing that I couldn't determine was why I was out here to begin with.

Until he came out of the treeline.

The one Miller had called Michael. The one with the light-brown hair and the freaky icy-blue eyes that weren't unlike Miller's.

Now we all knew why.

It wasn't a genetic anomaly at all.

My brain told me to go inside. To get the others, given that this crazy rapist was just outside the wards, but he stopped. He stopped at a spot where the wards wouldn't pick him up. He purposely stopped so that Miller and the guys wouldn't be alerted to his presence.

I'd have to put my faith in the wards, I supposed. Michael was here for a reason and didn't want anyone but me to know about it.

"My call came through the wards, I see," he said quietly, yet I heard him. It reminded me of how Miller had described the communication spell that Oliver created.

"What do you want?" I asked, assuming he'd hear me too, but I did take a few steps in his direction. There was still a lot of space between us, but I didn't want my voice to wake anyone in the house. If I could get this witch to leave without any of them knowing he'd been here, that was what I would do.

"I came to talk to you," he told me. "To help you understand."

"I already understand." My hands closed into fists at my sides with every spell I knew ready and waiting. They weren't much yet, but I'd use them. It also helped me control teleporting or whatever we were going to call it. I'd gotten good at not using it unless I wanted to, but I wasn't ready to test the theory.

"You don't. You're important, Hazel."

I sighed. "Yeah, yeah." Another few steps in his direction meant that I now had a better view. As far as I could tell, he was alone. Which was stupid of him, so I had to assume there were others lurking nearby. "I'm super important. I know. But the Fae was already here. He killed my parents and as far as I know, that debt is now paid. So..."

Michael gave a single nod. "That debt is now paid, but there were other reasons that I personally wanted you in our coven."

I snorted. "Which coven? Don't you belong to two?"

His face didn't change. "I only belong to one true coven. And Hazel, the Shadow Coven is the one true coven. In the end, we will win, so why don't you save the lives of your new friends and come willingly?"

My stomach turned. They'd kill everyone to get to me? It didn't make any sense. I wasn't special. I mean compared to regular people, sure. I had magic and could transport myself anywhere I wanted, or I would be able to once I figured out how to control that part. That made me special. But

I wasn't special among the witches. They all had cool abilities.

It had to be that damn angel blood that no one was even supposed to know about. But I wanted to be sure.

"Why?" I asked. "Why me? Why do you want me so badly?"

Michael tilted his head, like he was trying to figure out if I was telling the truth or not. After too long of a pause, he smiled. "I would've thought you figured that out by now. You're a means to an end, Hazel."

My stomach turned. That sounded like I was meant to be a sacrifice and I didn't like the sound of that at all. After swallowing back the acid burning my throat, I asked, "What does that mean? You want to sacrifice me to the moon or some stupid shit?"

"No," he said seriously. "I don't wish for your death, Hazel. I actually want you to live. The Fae wasn't going to kill you. Not right away, at least."

I snorted, feeling pretty snarky at the moment. "Right. He was going to drain me like a battery. That's so much better." I swallowed hard. "How do I save my friends?"

His smile grew as if he thought he had me right where he wanted me. "That's what I was hoping you'd ask." He almost took a step like he couldn't help himself and then remembered that if he came even an inch closer, the alarms would go off.

Now I wondered if there was anything to stop his magic from getting to me. I hadn't thought to ask that question.

"You save your friends by turning yourself over to me."

"Gross."

His eyes darkened. "Trust me when I tell you I don't want you like that. The deal with the Fae might be dead for the moment; however, you are still an important piece to the puzzle. An important part of an alliance between the Shadow Coven and the Fae realm. Your marriage was going to join us."

I shivered. "You sound like a mobster." I dropped my voice to mimic his. "'Your marriage will join the families.'" Then I went back to my normal voice. "No thanks. I have no interest in joining anything."

"Not even if it saves your friends?" He raised an eyebrow that I wished I could smack off his face.

Protecting Nellie and Gia was a top priority of mine. Oliver, Luken, Caleb, and Miller, too of course, but they were far better equipped to take care of themselves than the girls were.

"So, you thought I'd join your coven, complete your alliance, and... what?"

He took a deep breath. "You're wasting my time, but I'll entertain you. For now." For some reason, that last part sounded like a threat. "With the help of the Fae, the light covens of the world wouldn't stand a chance."

"World domination? That's what this is about? Are you serious right now? Because you sound like every bad guy in every movie."

He shook his head. "Not world domination, but absorbing the light power would be... beneficial."

That wasn't something I wanted to delve into any further. This whole thing was stupid. I wasn't going to turn myself over to Michael and his coven like some Mary Sue who was too stupid to live. I was going to rely on the guys to protect us and do my part as I could. But the more information I got out of this guy, the easier it might be for the guys to do just that.

"Well, you're going to have to find another way because I'm not coming with you."

"Not willingly, no. I understand that. But we already have witches embedded in the Echo Valley Coven. It would only take a simple spell for them to begin. No one would be left standing. Trust me,

Hazel." He sighed. "This has been planned for over twenty years."

Something about the way he'd said that this had been planned for twenty years didn't sit right with me. A new level of fear skittered up my spine and while I wouldn't let him know it was there, I also couldn't ignore it.

"Twenty-one years, maybe?" I cocked my head to the side and watched his reaction closely.

A sick smile played at Michael's lips. "They know then, do they?"

"We know." After all, I was one of Miller's family and the moment we could, I'd pledge myself to the Light Coven officially. "We know what you did. What your coven did."

"Then you should know why I personally want you in my coven."

At first, I didn't. I furrowed my brows trying to figure out what he meant. Then it hit me like a huge gust of wind threatening to take me off my feet.

"Miller?" I asked quietly, though I knew he'd hear me. "This is all about Miller?"

"There are many facets to our plan, Hazel. Nothing is all about one thing, but yes. I personally want Miller in my coven. Caleb will come back without my urging. I sent Miller to you because I knew how he felt about you. I knew he'd follow you anywhere. Even to the Shadow Coven. Father and sons fighting the light together? That's absolutely what I want. We'd be unstoppable."

"You're not going to get it." Miller's voice coming from behind me stiffened my spine. I didn't dare turn to look at him. His anger was radiating off his body and covering my skin like a hot blanket. I couldn't let his emotions take over mine, but it was hard to ignore and almost impossible to push away. "You should've woken me," he said quietly at my back and he was right.

"I didn't know why I was being drawn out here," I told him back.

"It doesn't matter, Hazel."

"Now that there's trouble in paradise," Michael said, causing both of us to turn our focus back to him. Other witches began stepping out from the woods. Michael took a step forward, which would have set off the ward to everyone else in the cabin.

Within moments, the rest of our people were around me. This wasn't a fair fight at all. Michael had more witches and I would've bet my ass that they were better trained.

"I know this little tiff won't last and the moment I

take Hazel, you will follow. I've always wanted my sons by my side."

Miller pushed forward so that he was blocking my view of the other witches. "You're not my father. I'm not your son. And I'll never fight alongside you. I highly doubt Caleb will either. In fact, I'm going to rip your throat out."

Michael chuckled. "Well, I already gave the order to attack Echo Valley," he said. My stomach tightened as a wave of nausea washed over me. "No one's coming to your aid."

Miller tensed. "I don't need anyone's help to kill you."

Before any of us could act, a large fireball descended and hit the corner of the cabin.

Fire rained down and it was all we could do to avoid it.

A ring of flames spread around the cabin and yard, encasing us and them inside so that no one could get out. I assumed Michael didn't know about my new ability and I was about to use it, but Luken grabbed my wrist.

"Don't," he said. "We have to end this. Be ready to take Nellie and Gia out of here if we tell you to."

Which meant the guys didn't want me to transport them. They were going to stay and fight no matter the cost.

I swallowed hard and tried to remember the spells I'd learned as the guys ran forward.

My life was burning down and I wasn't sure if I'd be a help or more of a hinderance.

But I wasn't going to stand there and watch.

MILLER

Now we were playing with fire?

This was going to be the last fight and however the chips fell at the end, it'd be with Hazel able to live out her life without the constant threat of the Shadow Coven. Michael and his coven could have their mission, but since it was to get to Hazel, I'd be the one standing in their way. Along with the line of people now beside me.

"What do you want to do?" Luken asked right before the Shadow Coven attacked.

A huge energy ball whizzed by us and hit the cabin. Several more followed. I pushed Hazel back, even though there was no way she was just going to stand there.

"Get Nellie and Gia out of here," I called out to her, then I turned and charged.

I wanted to get my hands on Michael. That was my only plan. The guys would have to fend off everyone else.

I threw spell after spell his way, which he quickly deflected. One of the Shadow Coven crossed my path. I slammed into him with the force of a freight train, bringing both of us to the ground. We each had a hold of the other witch, rendering our hands useless. Neither of us could cast a spell.

Fine by me. I had shit I was ready to take out on someone else.

In all the chaos, I lost track of the women and hoped Hazel had zapped them out of this.

Fuck. There was no winning here.

My fist connected with the witch's jaw. He was on top of me and snapped back quickly before coming back for me. We were on the ground and it took everything I had to keep him at arm's length. It was like he was possessed and his single mission was to kill me.

Suddenly, he was gone, flying through the air before hitting the ground with a bone-crushing thud. I looked up to find my dad standing there with his hand out. After putting mine in his, he yanked me to my feet.

"When did you get here?" I called over the noise.

"Just now. We knew something was happening. There was a fight in Echo Valley. We outed the Shadow Coven members hiding in our coven. Your mother saw their plans and here we are."

I looked to my left to see Mom casually casting a protection spell. It wasn't one that I'd seen her do before. Her arms flowed in a circle as the almost-invisible orb expanded.

"You brought her?" I asked.

Dad winced."Like she'd stay home." He grabbed me and threw me behind a tree right before a ball of energy flew past us. "What's the plan?"

"Fucking Michael." He'd know exactly what I meant.

"He's mine."

"Not if I get to him first." Though logically, it made sense that Dad would want to be the one to bring Michael to an end. As much as he'd done to the rest of us, he'd done the worst to Mom and Dad's sister. "Where's Hazel?" I pushed to my feet and scanned the scene.

The cabin was in flames. Energy balls from the dark witches flew across the field, hitting the trees and the cabin. This place wasn't going to be here when this was done. Oliver and Luken were throwing their own magic and Caleb had a dark witch in his hands. We were pitifully outnumbered, but that didn't matter to me.

"Did she get Nellie and Gia out of here?" I asked when I couldn't find her.

"I don't know. But we need to get back out there."

Dad ran to the right and I headed to the left.

I threw energy and spells at every witch I could get near. This felt like the epic end boss battle on every video game I'd ever played, yet there were only a couple dozen dark witches and the group of us.

It was loud. There was no way the closest humans weren't going to hear this, but we'd deal with that at a later time.

I was holding back the magic of one of the dark witches when I saw Hazel, Nellie, and Gia slink out from the other side of the burning cabin.

Fuck.

They should've left. And I couldn't keep an eye on them.

There was a moment that it occurred to me that we weren't going to win. That we were too outnumbered and outpowered. There were too many of them. And fucking Michael just sat back like the commander he always wanted to be with a group of witches whose only job looked to be protecting him.

It wouldn't help. It wouldn't stop us.

"Someone needs to get to the girls," I yelled, not thinking anyone would hear me.

Caleb did and he took off in that direction right as other members of our coven showed up to even the odds.

Suddenly, I was hit with a punch to the gut.

Fuck. That hadn't been a punch. It'd been a dark-energy spell. My skin burned like I'd been stuck with a hot poker. I fell and gritted my teeth.

Mom came to me and dropped to her knees. She didn't ask if I was all right because clearly, I wasn't. She pressed her hand to my stomach then yanked my shirt that was on fire up to the side. She mumbled some healing words and while it didn't fix the problem, I could at least breathe again.

"Fuck," I muttered as I slowly got to my feet. "Why didn't that kill me?"

Mom swallowed hard. "Michael wants you in their coven. I assume he gave an order that you could be hurt but not killed."

Yeah. Fuck that guy. But I'd use it to my advantage.

Without waiting for a break in the fight, I turned

to walk right through it when a loud, bloodcurdling scream ripped from someone's mouth.

It was Hazel. I felt that scream in my heart, which almost stopped right there.

Spinning around, I found her on her knees over something on the ground and took off in a run. If the Shadow Coven wasn't supposed to kill me, then I'd run right through all the magic. It was like slow motion and it took far too long to get to her.

When I did, my steps faltered.

Nellie lay on the ground with her head to her side and unfocused eyes.

She was dead.

Gia and Hazel both covered her body with their own and sobbed.

I hated to be a dick, but we didn't have time for this. Grieving for Nellie right now made them vulnerable. I came to a stop next to Caleb.

"I didn't get here in time," he said quietly.

"It's not your fault."

We'd deal with that later too.

I took Hazel by the shoulders and lifted her up. She pressed her face against my chest and I wanted to wrap her in my arms and take her away. Couldn't do that right now, though.

"Hey," I said as I moved her so that I could see

her face. "I'm so sorry, but we can't do this right now."

She looked up at me with watery, green eyes. "What?"

"There's still a fight going on." I motioned behind me to where my parents and coven were fighting for their lives. "We can't fall apart right now."

"But she—"

"I know. We will deal with this. Right now, I think you should get Gia out of here." That seemed like the best solution to me.

"But we—"

"Hazel," I snapped and I shook her little without meaning to. "Nellie is dead. You and Gia are in no condition to help. Go somewhere. Don't tell me where. You'll know when to come back." I pressed my hand against her chest and whispered the words that I needed. It connected us enough that she'd know when this was done. "Please go."

She quickly wiped under her eyes and gave me a little nod before wrapping herself around Gia and disappearing into nothing.

At least she'd be safe.

Caleb and I went back to the fight, but I only had one focus.

Michael.

I stomped toward him, using the energy from the earth to push away any dark coven witch who tried to stop me. There was only one way to end this and that was exactly what I was going to do. Caleb was there with me, handling any witch I didn't see until I was finally face to face with the man who'd hurt my mother. The dark witches that had been protecting Michael were needed on the battlefield.

"Miller," Michael said, as if this were a Sunday afternoon greeting at the park.

Caleb was standing guard against any other witch who might try to get in my way.

"You're going to die," I told him calmly. Now that we were here, the anger had started to dissipate, as if my subconscious knew that the release was about to happen.

Michael smiled as you would to a toddler who was being precious. "I don't think that will be happening today."

"You're wrong."

He narrowed his eyes. "And if I tell you that I have people tracking Hazel? That you sent her off on her own without protection?"

My heart stuttered, but my brain won out. There was no way anyone was tracking her right now. I didn't even know where she was, so he wouldn't be able to find her, either.

"Don't listen to him, Miller," Caleb called over his shoulder. "If you don't kill him, I will."

I took a step forward. "Threaten her again," I told him. "I don't even know why you got involved in that fucking deal her parents made, but you won't get another chance to hurt another woman."

One corner of his mouth turned up and I wanted to rain down fire on this man. "So you know. Then you understand that for me, this was never about Hazel. She was just a means to an end. If she joined our coven, you wouldn't be far behind. Then father and sons would be on the same side. As it should be."

My hand shot out like it had a mind of its own, wrapping around his throat. "I *am* on the same side as my father." He'd know exactly what I meant. "But there you go trying to use another woman for your own fucking needs." I tightened my grip, but he still looked undeterred.

There were so many ways I could've killed this man without even touching him. But I wanted to touch him. Wanted this to be as personal as it could get.

He'd hurt my mother. He'd hurt the woman I loved. He wasn't going to hurt anyone else.

"You're not going to do this," Michael said with a strained voice as I slowly tightened my grip. "Right now, you're torn. You want to kill me, but Hazel's out there on her own."

My grip loosened just the tiniest bit, which pissed me off. Hazel would be fine, I told myself. She had to be.

"*I'm* not torn." My dad's voice came from behind me right before he edged his way between Michael and me, which forced me to let go of the monster. "I'm not torn," he said again.

Before Michael could respond, my dad had a knife in his hand and thrust it into Michael's chest. Right below the ribcage and it was angled up.

My dad didn't want to chance Michael living through the attack.

Michael's surprised eyes looked down then at me as if I might save him. Fuck that. He was getting what he deserved. A gurgle came from his mouth right before the blood flowed out. Dad twisted the knife before pulling it out.

It was only a second before Michael fell to the ground and a pool of blood spread out around him.

That was going to take some cleanup.

"A knife?" I asked my dad.

"I wanted it to be personal." He set a hand on my shoulder. "Are you all right?" he asked. I nodded. "Hazel?"

"I made her take Gia out of here. Nellie's dead."

Dad closed his eyes slowly then opened them again. "We need to finish this."

I couldn't have agreed more. We fought those witches, but not for long. Soon enough, they were all either dead or trying to run off and other members of the Light Coven were on their track.

Once I knew this was over, I shut my eyes and thought of Hazel, sending out the vibe that it was all right to come back.

When I opened my eyes, she and Gia were standing before me, holding on to each other as if they were life rafts, both with red-rimmed eyes and splotchy, red skin.

This was going to be the hardest part of the whole thing.

Nellie was gone and she wasn't coming back.

20

HAZEL

WE LANDED with a *thud* on weak legs that couldn't hold us up. Gia and I both fell to our knees. My palms slid against the pavement, making scratches through my skin, but I didn't care. The pain in my hands was nothing compared to the pain in my heart.

"Nellie," Gia whimpered as she lowered her forehead to the ground.

It was odd. I'd only known Gia and Nellie a matter of weeks. I'd lost track of time and right now my brain wasn't firing on all cylinders. All I knew was that it hadn't been long, yet I loved them like they were family.

Now one of us was dead.

"We need to get up," I told her through my tears.

Tears that I hadn't shed for my own parents. Not like this anyway. After crawling over to Gia, ignoring the dig of the concrete into my knees, I wrapped an arm around her and said, "Gia, we have to get up. We're out in the open and I don't know if any of the dark witches can follow us."

Gia sniffed then shook her head. It took a lot of energy from both of us to get back on our feet.

I grabbed a hold of her shoulders while scanning the area around us. "Come on." With my arm around her, I led her away from the alleyway where we'd landed. Luckily, we weren't out in the open where just anyone could see us.

When we stepped out, I discovered that I'd brought us to a small tourist town up north. I'd gone there once with a friend when I'd been a kid and apparently, it was the only place I could think of when I'd needed to get Gia out of there.

Though I wasn't sure how I was as pulled-together as I was right then. We'd both just lost someone who was very important to us. I supposed I just knew that I couldn't break down. Someone had to have their head on straight right now.

There were a ton of people out on the side-walks, but I quickly found us a bench to sit on in the little park across from the alley where we'd landed. Once we were there, I blew out a slow breath.

"I can't believe she's dead." Gia sniffed then quickly brushed her fingers under her eyes. "I can't believe she died right in front of me."

"Me, either." I wrapped my arm around her shoulders and rubbed my hand up and down her arm as I fought off my tears. "What happened?" Because I had my back turned when Nellie fell."

"I don't know." Her voice was still watery with sadness. "We were doing the spells the guys taught us, then she yelled something at me and when I looked at her she was running toward me. Then one of those black energy balls hit her and she fell." She sniffed, barely able to finish her sentence. "I think she was trying to protect me."

"She would," I said softly. Nellie would've done anything to protect us, as we would have her.

Gia and I grew quiet as we each got lost in our own thoughts. I had no idea how much time passed as we looked out on the small park with kids playing as if there were no dangers lurking out there in the world. We knew better.

Dangers were everywhere.

A gentle warmness flooded me and flowed down my body like the best shower in the world. For some reason, that feeling filled my eyes with tears. For the first time, a quiet sob ripped from my chest.

Was this Nellie telling us she was OK? Was it some weird alert of danger? Nothing seemed out of place around me and it took far too long for me to realize it was Miller.

Before we'd transported out of there, he'd connected us. It wasn't strong and it wouldn't tell me much, but right now, it was telling me we could go back. At least that meant things were safer and he was alive.

Or I hoped it meant he was alive.

"We can go back," I told her quietly.

She shook her head. "I don't want to go back. I don't want to see her again. Not like that."

"I know," I said gently. "I don't want to, either, but I think Miller is telling us it's safe to come back." I was maybe three minutes from bursting out in tears right now and I really wanted to be with Miller when I did.

"Fine." She wiped the moisture from her cheeks. "Let's go back then." She swallowed hard as she stood.

It felt like we'd just gotten here, but if Miller was now calling us back, we must've been gone a while. We walked back to the alley so everyone in the park would see us before we wrapped our arms around each other as I closed my eyes, unable to hold back the tears now knowing that Miller was only moments away, then took a deep breath.

I pictured the cabin and him and everything we'd just left.

Next thing I knew, our feet hit the ground again, but this time, we were holding each other so tightly that we didn't collapse to our knees.

I looked up and found Miller, which had me falling into his arms, taking Gia with me.

Miller wrapped those strong arms around me and her, though he pulled me in much tighter to his body than he did her. Then he pressed his lips against the top of my head.

I turned to the side when I felt Gia being moved away from me. I didn't want to let go.

All I could do was watch as Luken took her into his own arms so that Miller could wrap his other one around me, which blocked my view. But I knew that Gia was being taken care of.

"Are you all right?" Miller asked against my ear.

All I could do was nod and let the tears fall. After I pulled myself together a little, I asked, "Is it over?" I pulled back so that I'd be able to see him. "Is the Shadow Coven gone?"

Miller's dad stepped forward with his mom right by his side. They both looked like they'd seen better days. Actually, as I glanced around, I saw everyone was dirty and disheveled. Much more so than when I'd taken Gia away.

"They're gone for now," Cooper told me. "Some ran off, but we have coven members hunting them down."

That was when I realized that we were literally surrounded by bodies. I took a step back. There was so much carnage all around us that my breath caught in my chest and acid burned my stomach.

"That's all going to be taken care of," Miller assured me. "We have... people who typically clean everything up."

What was this world I now belonged to?

Gia pulled herself away from Luken and if she hadn't looked so sad, I'd have also said she was blushing. I couldn't blame her. Luken was hot as hell. Not quite to Miller's level but still objectively hot. "What do we do now?"

"Go home." Caleb winced. Neither he nor Gia had a home to go to. "Well, they can go home."

"We're all going home," Eden told him as she stood before him. "You and Gia will come to our house. We have the extra rooms. We can figure everything else out from there."

"You guys go," Oliver said, looking at Miller and me. "Luken and Caleb will help me with Nellie."

Which meant they were doing something else with her than they would with the others. Right now, I just wanted away from the stench of death in the air, so when Miller took my hand to lead me toward where he'd left his car, I went. But I grabbed Gia to pull her along with us.

I didn't remember the drive back to Echo Valley. For all I knew, we'd been in the car either minutes or hours. It wasn't until we got to Miller's parents' house that I realized we'd left the woods.

"I need a shower." Gia gave me a sad smile as we got into the house with his parents right behind us.

"Me, too. I feel like I have seven years of dirt in my hair."

"How about Gia takes the shower upstairs?" Cooper offered. "Hazel can shower at Miller's and Eden, you hop in the one down here. There's still some clothes in the spare bedroom, Gia. That'll be yours."

She headed upstairs glumly and Miller led me out of the house, up the stairs outside, and into his apartment. I was in the bathroom with him undressing me as the water heated up. There was nothing sexual in his touch. It was all concern. But I wasn't going to break again.

Losing Nellie was awful and it was going to take some time to get past the pain of losing my friend, but it wouldn't break me.

When Miller stepped into the shower, I almost protested. I wanted him more than I wanted anything, but now wasn't really the time.

"I don't think—" I started, but he cut me off.

"I'm not going to do anything," he said quietly. "I just want to take care of you."

So I let him. He used a washcloth and soap to wipe away everything that had happened. At least the visible traces would be gone and it was nice to have him taking care of me.

There was still so much to get through, but for now, this was going to be enough. Us together would be enough.

Once we were done, he handed me a towel then wrapped one around his waist. I began drying myself off while he went out into the bedroom. I wasn't sure what else to call it, given the way his apartment was set up. It was like a studio apartment which meant it was kind of one room.

"Everything good?" I heard him ask someone,

but I didn't hear the response. I froze where I was until he came back in with some clothes for me. "Caleb's out there. He thought he'd shower here. Get dressed before you come out."

So I did.

We didn't wait for Caleb and went back to the house.

Soon enough, all of us were there picking at the food Eden had whipped up for us. Well, I picked. Gia picked. The guys went after it like starving street dogs who didn't know when they'd get their next meal. But my appetite just wasn't there.

"What'd you do with Nellie?" Gia asked and I'd been wondering too.

"We buried her in the coven cemetery," Oliver explained. "It's really only for witches actually in our coven, but Danna gave the go-ahead. It was the least the coven could do."

"I should've just given myself over to them," I said, though I hadn't planned on speaking those words out loud. "She'd be alive if I had. A lot of things would be different."

"Fuck that." Miller's voice was gentler than his words made it sound. "That wasn't the answer. We should've sent the three of you away when it all started. I stupidly thought you'd be safer with us."

"They probably were at first," Cooper confirmed. "Nellie was a tragedy that none of us could have prevented. She was trying to warn Gia."

"What do we do now?" I asked because I needed something settled. Anything.

"We'll have to rebuild the coven. Get you two"—he pointed at Gia and me—"into the coven as soon as possible and then you can figure out what you want to do. School, work, whatever."

"What about Juniper?" Gia asked me though she would've realized that I didn't have the answers.

"What about Nellie's boyfriend? Can we tell him that she's..." I looked at Miller with as much hope as I could muster.

"Do you have his name? Any information about him?" he asked but I could only shake my head. "I'm not sure what we could do then."

Luken cleared his throat. "If we can find Juniper, we can offer her sanctuary here. As long as she commits to the light. We can look for her though."

At least that was something.

"I was thinking." Eden leaned forward in her chair. "It seems we have some people who need somewhere to live. Caleb and Gia are welcome to our extra rooms for as long as they need them. No pressure."

"Are you comfortable with that?" I asked Gia.

She thought about that for a second then nodded. "I think I am. I don't have anywhere else I'd rather be and I want in the Light Coven immediately. If the Shadow Coven comes back, I want to be ready."

That made sense. "Well, maybe Gia could use the extra room for now and Caleb could have Miller's apartment."

"Uh..." Miller looked down at me with those icy-blue eyes that I loved on only him. "Where will be then, because, don't get me wrong, I like Caleb, but my apartment is small."

I sighed. "I assume that with my parents dead, I now own a big house. Once we get it situated, Gia could move in with us. Caleb too if that's what we want. The place is pretty big and unless my parents went on a spending spree since this all started, I also inherited a shit ton of money."

Miller snorted. "I hadn't thought of that. Yeah, if you're sure you want to live there."

"I am. I don't have the best memories, but we can make it something else. It's just going to need some work."

Miller smiled. "I can do work."

It was decided. Miller and I would stay in the

apartment until the house was ready. Gia and Caleb would stay with Miller's parents, which I secretly thought Cooper was most happy with. He had missed twenty-one years with his nephew and now was the time to catch up on that.

After a few hours, exhaustion set in for most of us. Oliver and Luken left to go to their own apartments while Gia and Caleb headed off to their own bedrooms. Eden yawned and, under Cooper's insistence, wished us a goodnight as we headed up to the apartment.

Miller locked the door behind us then wrapped me up in his arms.

"I'm so fucking glad you're all right," he said against my hair.

"I'm glad you're all right, too. When I left..." I shook my head. "I don't want to talk about any of that tonight. Do they have witch therapists because I feel like it's going to take years of therapy to get through it, but tonight, I just want to forget." I backed out of his arms and yanked my shirt over my head, then quickly undid my bra and dropped it to the floor. "Can you make me forget tonight?"

Miller gave me the smallest grin. "I'll make you forget everything." He slowly walked me back to until my legs hit the bed.

This way, I could get lost in the man I was never supposed to have yet loved with my whole heart.

"I love you, Hazel," he said once he had me pinned to the bed. "You're everything to me."

I ran a finger down the side of his face, where some bruises were starting to form. "I love you, too."

Then he spent what energy we both had proving it before wrapping me in his arms again.

It was the place I knew I was the safest and no matter what tomorrow brought, we'd be together and that was all that mattered right now.

I have a special treat on the next page! An exclusive BONUS scene featuring Miller and Hazel!

BONUS SCENE

Dear Reader,

I hope you enjoyed Fated Magic. Miller & Hazel really went through it but were always devoted to each other.

I have a bonus scene for you as a thank you for reading. Just click the link below, sign up for my newsletter, and you'll get an email with the bonus scene.

SIGN UP HERE:

https://geni.us/shadow-bonus

I you'd like to just keep up with my sales and new releases, you can follow me on BookBub!

Bookbub: https://www.bookbub.com/authors/heather-young-nichols

About the Author

Heather Young-Nichols is a USA Today Bestselling author of contemporary and paranormal romance. A native of the great and often very cold state of Michigan, she is better known at home and to her friends as the Snarker-in-Chief. A job she excels at beyond anything she could have imagined. She loves many things, but especially cold coffee, hot books, and baseball. But not necessarily in that order.

Find Heather on Social Media or by visiting her website.

heatheryoungnichols.com

facebook.com/heatheryoungnicholsauthor

instagram.com/heatheryoungnichols

amazon.com/Heather-Young-Nichols/e/B00KKTM54A

bookbub.com/authors/heather-young-nichols

tiktok.com/@heatheryoungnichols